the HORK-BAJIR
c h r o n i c l e s

The Yeerks are coming. . .
will you be next?
Flip the pages and find out.

Also by K.A. Applegate:

The Animorphs series

<MEGAMORPHS>

The Andalite Chronicles

the HORK-BAJIR chronicles

K.A. Applegate

AN
APPLE
PAPERBACK

SCHOLASTIC INC.

New York   Toronto   London   Auckland   Sydney
Mexico City   New Delhi   Hong Kong

ISBN 0-590-03646-7

Copyright © 1998 by Katherine Applegate. All rights reserved.
Published by Scholastic Inc.
SCHOLASTIC, APPLE PAPERBACKS, ANIMORPHS and associated
logos are trademarks and/or registered trademarks of Scholastic Inc.

12 11 10 9 8 7 6 5 4 3 2 1   9/9 0 1 2 3 4/0

Printed in the U.S.A.   40

First Scholastic paperback printing, October 1999

Cover painting by Romas Kukalis

For Michael and Jake

the HORK-BAJIR
chronicles

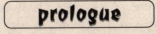

prologue

My name is Tobias.

I was restless. Don't ask me why, I just was. So I flew.

There were no Animorph missions planned. The others didn't need me right then. So even though the sun was going down, I flew.

I flew toward the mountains. Toward the secret, hidden valley the Ellimist had showed me.

Even now I had trouble finding it. Even though I knew exactly where it was. Even though, as a red-tailed hawk, I had vision far better than any human.

The Ellimist had concealed the valley from human eyes. How? Who knows? The Ellimist could hide all of planet Earth if he wanted to.

But knowing where the valley was, I could find it with some effort. I found the narrow gap between two ridges. I was not fooled by the way my eyes kept sliding away from the gap, as if some negative magnetism was at work.

I flew as the sun dropped and the air cooled and

the lift beneath my broad wings failed. I had to flap harder to stay aloft. Stupid, really. Now I'd have to spend the night here in the valley.

Then, below me, I saw a sight that made me glad to be there. A strange creature like nothing Earth has ever given birth to. It was four feet tall. There were razor-sharp blades at its ankles, knees, wrists, and elbows. There were two long, forward-raked horns coming from its head. It had a tail that ended in Stegosaurus spikes.

A young Hork-Bajir.

A young, *free* Hork-Bajir.

It was swinging, leaping through the trees like a monkey or a squirrel. Running through the tree branches, but happy-running, not scared-running.

I'd played a small part in the Ellimist's plan to create a free colony of Hork-Bajir. Not that the Ellimist interferes in the lives of other species.

So he claims.

Right.

In any case, the other Animorphs and I had played a role in helping two escaping Hork-Bajir find their way here. Jara Hamee and Ket Halpak. Like all Hork-Bajir, they had been infested by Yeerks. They'd been slaves of the Yeerks.

Somehow they had escaped. Don't ask me how. Ask the guy who doesn't interfere in the lives of other species.

They'd had a baby. That was him . . . or her . . . cavorting beneath me. I still was not very good at telling the difference.

Hork-Bajir don't live as long as humans. So they grow up faster, too.

I increased my speed and outraced the Hork-Bajir child. I found the nest of caves, six or eight, all close together, where we'd figured the Hork-Bajir would live.

But to my surprise I could now see that the caves were unused. The adults were in the trees. But not just Jara Hamee and Ket Halpak. There were a dozen or more Hork-Bajir there now. All free. Many starting to raise families.

I realized then that I had not accidentally headed toward the hidden Hork-Bajir valley. It had been deliberate, even if it was subconscious. I'd been feeling kind of down. But now, seeing this fragile community of free Hork-Bajir . . . well, how can you see freedom replace slavery and not feel good?

These Hork-Bajir had been the unwilling shock troops of the Yeerk Empire. Now they were raising families, carefully stripping the bark from the trees, building a fire near the cave entrances.

I swooped down, down through the branches of a huge elm tree. Jara Hamee was in the high branches.

<Hi, Jara,> I said.

He waved. He smiled. Or what passes for a Hork-Bajir smile. Actually, it's an expression that would make you want to run, screaming "Mommy! Mommy!" if you didn't know what it was.

The workday was about done for the Hork-Bajir. They invited me to the fireside as the night rolled over the valley and the stars appeared.

Like any wild bird, I'm a bit leery of fire. But I found a comfortable perch on a fallen log. Near enough to enjoy the light. Far enough not to feel too much heat.

I was welcomed like more than a friend. The Hork-Bajir think I liberated them.

Hork-Bajir are simple creatures. Not exactly the geniuses of the galaxy, I suppose. Talking to Jara Hamee can be like talking to a four-year-old. But they are decent, sweet creatures. Almost timid, despite their nightmarish appearance.

"Eat bark? Good bark," Jara Hamee said, offering me a slab.

<No, thank you,> I said. <I don't want to keep you all awake if you're ready to sleep.>

"Sleep?" Ket Halpak said. "No sleep. Tell story."

Now, I hated to even think what a Hork-Bajir story might be like. Let's face it, sweet or not, Hork-Bajir are not big talkers.

<What stories do you tell?> I asked, cringing a little at the possibilities. I felt like I was asking Great-

grandma to tell me about her youth, you know? Like the result wasn't exactly going to be *Party of Five*.

"Story of Father Deep. Story of Mother Sky," Ket Halpak suggested.

"Story of *Jubba-Jubba*," another Hork-Bajir said.

But Jara Hamee looked shrewdly at me. Well, once again, what passed for shrewd.

"Story of Yeerks and Andalites," he said. "Story of war."

That perked up my interest.

The others all nodded.

"My father-father was a seer," Jara Hamee said. "Different. Not like other Hork-Bajir. Not like Jara Hamee and Ket Halpak. Like . . . like Tobias. Seeing far. Knowing much. Father-father learn story of Andalite. Learn story of Yeerk. Give story to Jara Hamee father. Jara Hamee father give story to Jara Hamee."

<I'd like to hear the story of the Hork-Bajir war with the Yeerks,> I said.

I don't know what I expected. I guess I figured Jara would say something like, "Yeerks come. Bad. Fighting. Yeerks win. We lose."

But that wasn't it at all. Jara Hamee closed his eyes and began rocking back and forth. A weird gargoyle, bright orange and deep shadow in the firelight.

He rocked for several minutes, while everyone waited patiently.

And then he started to tell his tale. It was in the rough, stilted, limited speech of the Hork-Bajir. A mix of English and Hork-Bajir and languages I could only guess at. It was hard to follow at first. But I swear after a few minutes the words grabbed hold of my brain somehow. I could not only hear the guttural words, I could hear the original words as spoken by Jara Hamee's father-father. And the others who played a part in the story.

An Andalite female named Aldrea.

A Yeerk named Esplin.

The Hork-Bajir seer, Dak Hamee.

Maybe it was the firelight, or the way Jara rocked back and forth as if he were in a trance. But I soon forgot where I was. I was far away.

Far, far away.

I settled onto my branch, fluffed my feathers against the cold, and listened.

chapter 1

Andalite date: year 8561.2
Yeerk date: Generation 685, mid-cycle
Hork-Bajir date: early-warm
Earth date: 1966

ALDREA

My name is Aldrea-Iskillion-Falan. I am an Andalite. A female.

That was all there was to say about me back then. But later I became much more. My name became a cruel joke among my people. And later still, a curse.

But when this story began, I was just a young female. Just Aldrea. Not yet *the* Aldrea.

I understood very little back then, listening with my mind to the thought-speak shouts and curses around me. I only knew that something terrible had happened.

I knew that the young, powerfully built Andalite

warrior who had burst in upon the prince was angry. More than angry. Furious.

His name was Alloran-Semitur-Corrass. He would play a role in my life and the life of the galaxy. But back then, all I knew was that he was enraged.

<Yes, it's confirmed. Yes, Prince Seerow, it has happened. As I *warned* you it would.>

The Andalite warrior was pacing back and forth, whipping his tail impatiently. He was angry. He was bitter.

<But it can't be,> the other Andalite said softly. <They promised me. They gave me their word. They . . .>

<I have visual logs,> Alloran snapped. He opened his hand and revealed a small cylinder. A holographic recorder. He gave the instruction. <Play.>

Before our eyes a three-dimensional picture appeared. It was dark. The focus was imperfect. But we could see Gedds loping in their awkward way. The Gedds carried weapons. Knives. Clubs. Primitive weapons. But one of the Gedds carried something more dangerous: an Andalite shredder.

In the distance, beyond the Gedds, were four Andalite warriors. They were joking, relaxing a bit, killing time. Soldiers doing dull, uninteresting duty and making the best of it.

One Andalite spotted the advancing Gedds.

<Hold fast,> he called.

The Gedds kept moving. The Gedd with the shredder held it concealed behind his back.

<Hold fast, Yeerks. You are not allowed closer to the ships.>

I peered into the flickering hologram. Yes, I could see a parked Andalite fighter. The other ships and warriors were not visible.

<I said, hold fast!> the Andalite warrior said.

<Orders are to avoid incidents,> another Andalite said. <Don't you know these parasites are our brothers?> This was said with a sneer.

The Gedds moved closer.

<Orders or not, these filthy slugs are not touching my ship.>

And then, as if in slow motion, I saw the Gedd pull the shredder from behind his back.

TSEEEEW!

TSEEEEW!

Even in hologram, the light was blinding. Two Andalite warriors were incinerated.

The two remaining warriors drew their weapons and arched their tails, but it was too late. A wave of Gedds descended on them, weapons raised.

The hologram flickered off.

Prince Seerow slumped, his upper body leaning forward, his four legs appearing weak, as he absorbed the awful truth.

Prince Seerow, whose name was to become a curse word and a joke.

He was my father.

<They gave you their word?!> Alloran practically shrieked. <Their *word*? They're parasites. The Yeerks steal the bodies of other species. What did you expect of them?>

<They have no history of harming intelligent life-forms. The Gedds are barely conscious in their natural state,> Prince Seerow argued. <It's not as if they were stealing the bodies of truly sentient creatures. They and the Gedds are symbiotic. They have —>

Alloran stepped closer to my father. <Listen to me, my prince.> The word "prince" was said with a sneer. <Approximately four hundred Gedds attacked our ground base last night. They overwhelmed the two dozen Andalite warriors on duty there. The two dozen Andalite warriors who had been specifically ordered *not* to fire on Gedds.>

<They were never a threat before,> Prince Seerow said. <The Yeerks, even the ones in Gedd hosts, are harmless. I didn't want our warriors to accidentally —>

4

<These four hundred harmless Gedds — these Yeerks, I should say, because they were all certainly Yeerk-controlled — butchered my warriors,> Alloran said.

My father turned away. He directed his main eyes and his stalk eyes away, unwilling to look Alloran in the face.

<*Butchered*, Prince Seerow,> Alloran said. <Shall I show you the holos of the aftermath? These were the gentlest pictures. I have others. Would you like to see what they did to the bodies of my warriors?>

Now it was something other than anger in Alloran's tone. I could feel the pain in his hearts. And the guilt. The guilt of having survived, while his friends died.

I don't know how I understood him so well. I was very, very young. So young that neither of the adults paid any attention to my eavesdropping. I was very young then, but I had an active imagination. Maybe that was how I could so clearly imagine the awful scene of Alloran stepping over the bodies. . . .

I shuddered. It must have been terrible. And I shuddered for another reason, too: I knew, young though I was, that my father would be blamed.

<These four hundred Gedds overwhelmed my warriors,> Alloran said, building back to anger again. <And then they seized the four attack fight-

ers and two transports that were on the ground at the time.>

<Couldn't they be intercepted in orbit?> my father asked.

<No. You see, there was no warning. My warriors were dead before they could call for help or give warning.>

<Still, four fighters and a pair of slow transports . . . our forces should have no trouble catching them.>

<Catch them? They've escaped into Zero-space,> Alloran said. <Four hundred Yeerk-infested Gedds with shredder-armed fighters.>

Two young warriors came rushing in. We were inside one of the shelters we were forced to use on this planet. There were large windows, certainly, but still, it was an enclosed space, and like any Andalite I found it disturbing.

One of the young warriors had a terrible slash scar down one flank. It had been treated, but you could see the wound was still fresh.

<Prince Seerow,> the wounded warrior said. <Remote orbital sensors show that the two transport ships did not immediately jump to Zero-space. They landed on the far side of the planet.>

Alloran practically leaped at the young warrior. <Are they still on the ground?>

<No, sir. Sensors show they stayed on the ground for only an hour. Then they returned to orbit and jumped to Z-space.>

<Prince Seerow,> the other young warrior said, <they landed beside major Yeerk pools. They apparently loaded a large number of Yeerks before escaping.>

<A large number? Estimates?> my father demanded bleakly.

<The computer estimate is that with advance planning and careful coordination, they may have embarked as many as a quarter million Yeerks.>

<A quarter million?> My father gasped. <But . . . but the Yeerk leaders. . . . They have been my friends. They cannot know about this! The Council of Thirteen must not have known. This is some rebellion, some group of malcontents.>

<Fool,> Alloran said.

My father's head jerked as if Alloran had tail-whipped him. It was impossible! A lowly warrior calling a prince "fool"!

<You fool,> Alloran said again. <You coddled them. You trained them. You showed them the universe. You showed them all the things they could not have, living here on this planet of theirs. You even built them portable Kandronas and thus freed them.>

<The Yeerks are intelligent, sentient creatures.

7

They have a right to join other sentient races. They have a right —>

<A quarter million highly intelligent, ruthless, and determined parasites have just been loosed upon the galaxy,> Alloran said flatly. <They have six Andalite ships. How long before they learn to build their own ships? How long before they become a plague? How long till they find some race more useful than the Gedds, some race they can infest and transform into shock troops? There are thousands of inhabited planets in just this arm of the galaxy.>

Alloran turned all four of his eyes on my father. <Prince Seerow, you are relieved of duty.>

<You can't relieve me!> my father cried.

<When a commander has become incapacitated due to injury or mental defect, his subordinates may relieve him,> Alloran quoted from the regulations.

<What mental defect?> my father demanded.

<Stupidity,> Alloran said harshly. <The stupidity of kindness. Charity to potential enemies. You're a fool, Seerow. A soft, sentimental, well-meaning fool. And now my men are dead and the Yeerks are loose in the galaxy. How many will die before we can bring this contagion under control? How many will die for Seerow's kindness?>

Seerow's Kindness.

Even then, all those years ago, I knew. My father's epitaph had just been written.

I could not watch anymore. I ran outside, unnoticed by the adults. I ran outside into the Yeerk twilight. The wild green and yellow-streaked sky was turning dark.

The harsh air rasped in my throat. Soon the nightly rain, the acid rain, would fall and I would have to retreat back into the shelter.

We would be leaving this planet soon. I knew that. I could see the remaining warriors setting up a defense perimeter around our small compound.

The Andalite-Yeerk Peace and Cooperation Center. That's what it was called. And now it was beginning to bristle with shredder cannon.

I turned my stalk eyes toward the Yeerk pool. The Yeerks called it Sulp Niar. It looked like molten lead.

I had come to the Yeerk planet with my mother and father. It was all part of showing the Yeerks that we were sincere in our desire for peace and friendship.

But I had never liked this planet. I had never liked the Yeerks. And now they had destroyed my father's dreams.

Seerow's Kindness.

My father's love of peace had released the evil of war on an unprepared galaxy.

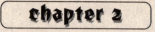

chapter 2

Andalite date: year 8563.5
Yeerk date: Generation 686, early-cycle
Hork-Bajir date: late-cool
Earth date: 1968

ALDREA

I am the daughter of Prince Seerow. My friends tease me sometimes. They call me "Seerow's *Un-*kindness."

You see, I'm not like most females. I'm not content to stay within the sciences and the arts, the traditional female occupations. I don't want to be a Zero-space theorist or a grass-scape designer or a cloud artist.

I want to be a warrior. I want to fight the Yeerks.

I know what everyone says: Females are not born to be warriors. We have smaller tail blades. More like scalpels than like the great, curved scythes our brothers have.

But tail fighting isn't everything. Not in modern

war, which is fought with shredders and ionic-dispersion explosives launched from our most advanced ships. The war against the Yeerks won't be about tail fighting.

Besides, with the very recent invention of morphing technology, we can fight using any number of physical bodies. And, many studies have shown that females are actually superior when it comes to morphing.

No one listens. Not my own mother. Not even my father.

Of course, my father doesn't listen to much of anything anymore. He does whatever small, out-of-the-way, humiliating job he's given. He does what he's told.

Which was why we were just coming into orbit above an irrelevant planet no one cared about. It was an exile, sort of. My father was being sent where he could do no harm.

<Transparent,> I told the computer. The outer bulkhead in my cabin turned from blank gray to clear. Outside I could see black space blazing with stars. But filling half my view was the planet itself. Our new home.

For the most part it looked more like some dead moon than a living planet. Much of the surface was dark gray, sterile rock. I knew from our briefing that there was only a very thin atmosphere. It was cold.

Bitterly cold. With air so thin that an Andalite could expect to suffocate and die within thirty minutes.

But around the equator of the planet was a strange sight: huge, deep rifts, interwoven, interconnected. It looked as if someone had stepped on the planet, squashing it like a ripe ooka melon so that the sides had burst open.

In fact, that's exactly what had happened. Millions of years earlier, a massive asteroid had hit the planet's northern pole. The impact had shattered the crust, especially around the equator. It had opened massive valleys that cut deep, deep into the planet's surface.

Valleys with steep, rugged walls. The valleys were as much as fifty miles deep and held onto a rich nitrogen-oxygen atmosphere. The walls of the valleys were green. The floors of the valleys were a poisonous, eerie blue. Our sensors did not penetrate that blue mist.

As we slid across the night–day line into darkness, I could see that the blue glowed.

I stared down at the planet for a long time. Till finally someone sent my brother to get me. The door of my cabin trilled.

<Yes, come in,> I said. And to the computer, I added, <Opaque.> The wall turned flat gray again.

My brother stuck his upper body in. <What are you doing? Let's go! Didn't you hear the announce-

ment? The surface ship is waiting. Let's move it, let's move it!>

<I'm coming, Barafin, I'm coming,> I said heavily.

<Did you look at the planet?> Barafin asked. <Weird-looking, isn't it?>

<It's an unusual place,> I agreed. <But I guess it will be okay. Mother and Father will take care of us. It won't be so bad.>

<All my friends are like two hundred light-years away,> Barafin said. <We'll be the only Andalites on the planet.>

<We'll be okay,> I said.

<Yeah, I guess if this planet were dangerous they wouldn't have sent Father.>

I should have told him to stop talking that way. But I didn't. He was right. Barafin barely speaks to my father. Barafin has taken a lot of teasing from the other kids at school. So have I. But I think it hurts Barafin more.

I said good-bye to the little cabin that had been my home for two months of travel from the Andalite home world to this nowhere planet. I had already packed up my few personal belongings. My holo of our scoop back on the home world, the Pakka doll my mother had given me when I was a child, the wish-flower I'd kept from when we were hoping to have Barafin.

A sullen pilot flew us down to the surface. We

descended through the thin upper atmosphere, skimmed across the gray barrens, and then dropped down inside one of the massive impact valleys.

The view through the windows of the shuttle was amazing. One second we might as well have been skimming the surface of a very large asteroid. The next second we were surrounded by trees.

The size of the valley defied description. There was nothing even close on the home world or on the Yeerk world. The vegetation was sparse and scruffy toward the top of the valley, up where the air was thinnest. As we descended, mile after mile downward, the trees grew taller, the plants more lush. Pressing against the window to see straight downward, I saw that the lushness gave way to lurid, wild-colored plants nearer the poisonous blue bottom of the valley.

Down there, things grew fuzzy and indistinct as the atmosphere thickened to the point of becoming opaque.

We headed for a landing in a clearing in the trees. We were perhaps thirty miles below the lip of the valley. And another fifteen or twenty miles above the simmering, steaming blue.

I kept thinking we were almost down. But then I realized my whole perspective was distorted. The trees, which I'd expected to be normal-sized trees, were huge. The smallest must have been two hundred feet tall. The largest were ten times that high. Two thousand feet tall! With trunks a hundred feet in diameter.

The valley walls were mostly very steep. Often the rising ground was no more than a few dozen yards away from the midpoint of one of the magnificent trees. Branches extended from the trunk over to the edge of the sloped ground. But in the other directions, out over the valley, the branches extended for insane distances.

<Serious trees,> Barafin commented.

<The largest trees ever discovered on any planet,> our mother said, her eyes bright. She's a biologist. For her this was great: a mostly unexplored planet full of unclassified plants and animals. I know she felt sorry for my father, but at the same time, this was like paradise to her.

We landed in the small clearing. No more than a thousand yards of grass, some of it almost level.

Four crew members began unloading our supplies and equipment. And I stepped out for the first time on the planet that was merely called Sector 5, RG-21578-4.

RG meant red giant. That was the type of sun at the center of this system. The dash-four meant this was the fourth planet from that sun.

<I thought there was a sentient species on this planet,> I said as we stepped gingerly out onto un-

tasted grass. <I didn't see any sign of them as we were coming down.>

<They aren't a city-building or road-building species,> my father said, trying to sound upbeat. <They are quite primitive, according to the data from the robot probes. Their appearance can be very fearsome, but they are harmless, gentle herbivores. Not especially bright, I'm afraid,> he added. <No culture to speak of. No written language. No music, as far as we know. They don't build much, if anything. And they are technologically the equivalent of a primordial civilization.>

<So why are we here?> Barafin grumbled, rolling his stalk eyes upward to encompass the monstrous size of the closest tree.

<We are here to make contact with the population and make sure that the Yeerks are not moving against these people,> my father said.

Barafin laughed. <Why would the Yeerks be interested in this place?>

One of the crew members was standing nearby. <They wouldn't be,> he said. <No one's interested in this place.> He shot an openly insolent look at my father.

He might as well have added, <That's why Prince Seerow has been assigned here: because it's a meaningless planet where the fool will do no harm.>

My father ignored him. But I could see that the unspoken insult had reached him. His nostrils flared. His main eyes widened. For a moment I thought he might put the jerk in his place. But then, as I'd seen so often before, my father sagged, turned away, and accepted the humiliation.

<At least the grass tastes okay,> Barafin said, digging his hoof into the blue-green grass.

I looked around at the planet of trees. How those huge trees weighed me down. I felt the radical slope of the ground beneath my hooves. It made one feel as if one might fall over and never be able to stop rolling and rolling and rolling.

I thought it was an awful place, despite its oversized beauty. <What should we call this place?> I asked. <We can't keep calling it Sector Five, RG-Two-One-Five-Seven-Eight-Four.>

<We follow the usual practice of naming a planet after its sentient species,> my mother said.

<I've forgotten. What are these more-or-less sentient creatures?>

<They are called Hork-Bajir,> my father said. <This is the home world of the Hork-Bajir. Soon we will get a chance to meet one.>

I saw something moving, coming around the base of the closest tree.

<Very soon, I think.>

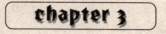

chapter 3

DAK HAMEE

My name is Dak Hamee.

I am Hork-Bajir. But I am different. Not like others. I have known this since I was too small to strip any but the most tender bark.

My mother said to me, "Dak Hamee, you are strange."

She took me to see the elders in the Tribe Tree. They looked at me. They spoke to me.

"He is strange," Elder Mab Kahet said.

"Yes, he is strange," Elder Ponto Fallah said.

"He is a 'seer,'" Mab Kahet said. He was not happy. He was not sad. He was . . . disturbed.

"What is a 'seer'?" my mother asked.

The Old One, Tila Fashat, opened her toothless mouth and said, "A seer is one who is born to show a new way. Many, many seasons pass, then our father, the Deep, and our mother, the Sky, say, 'Send a seer to the people. The people have need.' And so one is born who is different."

18

"My son is different," my mother said heavily.

"Yes," the Old One said. "He is different."

I am Dak Hamee. I am different. I am the seer. I am to show my people a new way.

But I did not know the new way. The Old One said I would know when the Deep and the Sky told me. They would tell me what to do.

Until then, I had to wait. Sometimes I thought about things that no Hork-Bajir thinks about: What is really within the Deep? How high is the Sky?

Sometimes I would take a small piece of burned wood from the fire. I used it to make markings on the smooth wood where the bark had been stripped. I made markings that look like rocks. Or trees. Or like the *Jubba-Jubba* monster that lives in the Deep. Once I made markings that looked like my friend, Jagil Hullan.

"This is you, Jagil," I said.

"That is not me," Jagil said.

"Yes. See that the wrist blades are shaped like your wrist blades. See that the tail is like your tail. See that the horns are short, like your horns."

"That is not me," Jagil said. "I am me. I am here. I am not there. I am not a scraping by a burned stick."

I tried to explain. But Jagil did not understand.

Maybe he was right. Maybe I was only being different again.

One day I was harvesting in the high branches of an old *Siff* tree. I stripped the bark with my leg blades, and held a branch with my hands. I looked up at Mother Sky. I wondered again how high she was.

But then, there was something different in the Sky. It was not the sun. It was not a moon. It was smaller. It was shiny. It was shaped like an egg, but with branches.

It was coming down from the Sky.

I knew that this was Mother Sky speaking to me. I knew that this different thing was sent to me. It was different. I am different.

I climbed down the tree to the ground. I walked toward the place I saw the Sky-thing going.

It was on the ground. And there were creatures.

Not any of the monsters of the Deep. Not any of the lizards or snakes of the Outside. They had four legs. One, two, three, four. They had a tail, but it was high, not dragging the ground. They had two arms. They had no blades, except one small blade on each of their tails. Their horns were very small. And they moved. And there were eyes on the ends of their horns.

They were not horns. Horns do not have eyes.

They had no mouths. They looked at me with four eyes.

I walked closer to see them. They did not move. They only watched.

"I am Dak Hamee," I said.

They did not speak. They only stared.

"I am Dak Hamee," I said again.

<I am Prince Seerow.>

The voice was in my head! It made no sound. But I heard it! It was strange. The words were not words of the Hork-Bajir. But I understood them.

"I am Dak Hamee," I said again.

<It's a juvenile,> one of the creatures said. <Probably about equivalent in age to Aldrea or Barafin. Aldrea? Barafin? Maybe you should speak with him.>

<Not me!> a new voice said. <He's covered in blades!>

But one of the creatures stepped toward me. <My name is Aldrea,> she said. <We are Andalites. We would like to be your friends.>

Suddenly, I knew that my waiting was over. This was the new thing I had been created for. This was what I had to understand, so that I could show my people the way.

This was why Father Deep and Mother Sky had made me a seer.

chapter 4

DAK HAMEE

I did not stay with the four-legged strangers. I ran away. I went back to my mother. She took me to the elders.

The Old One said, "This is why Dak Hamee was born. This is why Father Deep and Mother Sky have sent us a seer. Dak Hamee must watch and speak. Then he must show us the way."

So I went back to the strangers.

There were only four now. The egg-shaped flying thing was gone. They had dug into the valley wall. It was not deep, but they had covered the scooped area with a cloth that hung in the air.

When the rain fell or Mother Sky made lightning, they stayed in this place. Other times they stood or ran on the grass. They had other things. Things without names that glowed like Father Deep. And things that made sounds in my head. And things that did nothing at all.

I went to them with Jagil. Jagil was afraid.

"We should not go there," he said.

"We should," I said. "I must watch and listen."

"We can climb a tree and watch."

"No. These creatures do not climb. They walk on the ground. So we must walk on the ground, too."

Jagil was afraid. But Jagil came with me. We went into the clearing. The strangers looked at us.

<Hello,> one said, making the sound that was only in my head.

"I am Dak Hamee," I said.

"I am Jagil Hullan."

<Not enough for the universal translator,> one of the strangers said. <We need more words before it can begin to translate.>

One of the strangers, the smaller one with the smaller tail blade, pointed at herself. <I am Aldrea. I am an Andalite. I spoke to you before. Do you remember?>

<Tell you one thing,> the other smaller stranger said. <You don't want to have to fight these Hork-Bajir. Those blades look very serious.>

<They're peaceful, not violent.>

I didn't know what to say. It was confusing. "Welcome, Aldrea," I said. "Welcome, Andalite."

<Not exactly chatty, are they?>

The one called Aldrea came forward. With her hand she pointed at the closest tree. <Tree,> she said.

I understood her. Her words were in my head. But the words themselves were strange. I did not know these words. Still I understood their meaning.

"Tree. *Stoola* tree," I said, in my own words. The stranger called Aldrea nodded. She wanted to know more about the tree.

I knew about this tree. "The bark below the lowest branch is too old. Hard to eat. The bark above the lowest branch but before the *mislit* is good. But harvesting it is bad. This bark helps the *Stoola* tree to grow new *Stoola* trees. Only the bark above the *mislit* may be taken. This is the Truth given to us by the Old One."

<Got it,> one of the others said. <Translation is effective at sixty-four percent. Coming online now.>

<We can understand you now,> Aldrea said.

"I understand you."

<Yes, that's because thought-speak works with universal symbols as well as with specific words,> an older stranger said.

I looked at her. I was confused.

<My love, I think perhaps this is a case where we should allow the young ones to communicate. Aldrea seems better able to communicate with young Dak Hamee than you or I are. This young Hork-Bajir is not an official. I think this is an informal contact.>

<Be careful, Aldrea. You, too, Barafin. Don't lose sight of the scoop.>

Aldrea came and stood closer. Barafin did, too. Jagil was nervous. He wanted to run away. But if I did not run, Jagil would not run.

"Where is your Tribe Tree?" I asked Aldrea.

<Not here,> she said. <On another planet.>

I nodded. "Yes. Not here. What is another planet?"

<Do you see the stars at night?> she asked me.

"When Mother Sky is dark, she shows us her flowers."

<Well, each of those flowers is a star. Like your own sun. Only very far away.>

Jagil said, "No."

But I said, "Sun is sun. Mother Sky's flowers are flowers."

<They may look like bright flowers. But they are suns. Hundreds of suns. Thousands. Mil . . . I mean that there are more stars than there are trees. They look small because they are far away.>

I heard these words. And these words made me think very hard. But then . . .

"Yes," I said suddenly, amazed. "Yes! Things that are far away look small. This is true."

"Far is far," Jagil said, looking alarmed.

<These stars are very, very far away,> Aldrea said. <And around some of these stars are planets. Like this place. Other places with very different trees. And different creatures.>

I felt . . . I did not have words for how I felt. Things that are far away seem small. Even when they are large. This idea was like an exploding seed pod in my head.

Things that are far away seem small. If Mother Sky's flowers are very far away, they might be very large. They might be . . . suns!

My legs became weak. I rested back on my tail. I could not speak.

"Are you sick?" Jagil asked me.

<We come from one of those stars,> Aldrea said.

"How . . . how can you come from so far?"

<We flew,> she said.

Mother Sky's flowers were suns. And these strangers had come from one of those suns. The things I thought were true were no longer true.

I felt . . . I felt that I wanted to know more. This feeling was not new. But now I felt that this delicate stranger could help me. I could know so many things! So many things!

On that day, the old Dak Hamee died. On that day I truly became Dak Hamee, the seer.

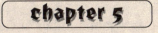

ESPLIN 9466

My name is Esplin 9466.

I come from no regular Yeerk pool. I was born from the decaying bodies of my tripartite parents, along with several hundred brothers and sisters, aboard ship. And one twin, naturally, as you know from the double-number designation.

I have never lived on the home world. I was born in a sterile, titanium-alloy tank, beneath the warmth of a portable Kandrona.

It was all I knew.

Older Yeerks spoke of the pools of home. Of their smells and temperatures; of their size and spaciousness; of their traditions that stretched back for hundreds of generations.

My pool was simple and crude. It had been constructed using the host bodies of Gedds. Gedds are imperfect hosts. Even so, I wished we had more of them.

But there were no host bodies available, not on

27

this spacecraft. So we lived in our pool. As simple Yeerks must. And I would have lived happily enough.

But then came the day when it was my turn to take "training."

There were a certain number of Gedds, often old or crippled in some way, that we used as training hosts. We were given fifteen minutes to enter the host body, take it, and then release the host body and leave.

Fifteen minutes. It was all the time allowed with so many untrained Yeerks and so few available hosts.

We lined up in the pool six at a time. I was fourth in line. I waited impatiently, afraid. I admit it: afraid. You hear stories about what it's like. About the hallucinatory sensory input. About the strange sensation of having another mind under your control. About the extension of your own body through unfamiliar limbs.

But you don't know till you do it.

When it was my turn, the Gedd's head was thrust beneath the surface of the pool. My sonar found the head quite easily, of course. And I'd been taught how to pinpoint the opening into the head by extending two palps.

It was quite a small entryway. I had to squeeze

myself down and work my way slowly inside the ear canal. From there on, it was all by feel. My sonar didn't work, of course. And the smells I encountered were unfamiliar, useless.

But then, after what seemed far too long a time, my palps encountered a surface alive with electricity!

The brain. I could feel the activity, the snapping neurons, the arcs of microvoltage between synapses. I had to flatten myself all the way. My palps sought for trenches, gaps, openings around the brain. And I found them. I pushed my body down inside each wrinkle of the brain. Just as I'd been taught to do.

And slowly at first, then faster and faster, I began to make contact! I felt the neurons connecting to me!

Only someone who has done it can understand. It was . . . it was beyond description. Suddenly, I was not just myself, I was something much larger. Where my body ended, a second body began, so that very soon I forgot my own body entirely.

I had arms many times longer than myself. They ended in three-fingered hands that could actually move objects. Lift them, turn them over, set them down in different ways. I had legs that lifted my new body up high. I could move through the air!

Oh! How can I explain it? The power! The joy! The feeling that I had suddenly grown huge, vast, powerful.

No one had told me it would be so wonderful.

And then I felt inside the brain, a place I had not been. A place untouched by my control.

I opened that part of the brain. And in doing so, I opened the Gedd's eyes.

For a long, frozen moment of disbelief, I did not know what was happening. I didn't understand what my brain was receiving.

How could I? How could any Yeerk who has not had a host?

Sight!

Objects — not felt, not smelled, not reflected on sonar — but *seen*. It was like a sonar image, but oh, so much more. So much! The data assaulted my brain. I reeled, overwhelmed, unable to understand or accept.

I looked through the Gedd's eyes. I used the Gedd's own brain to filter and interpret the eerie, insane input. And then, slowly, I understood.

I was looking at other Gedds.

I was looking around at the inside of the spacecraft.

I was looking down at my own pool.

So small, it was. So dark. So . . . insignificant.

I saw movement within the pool and caught a flash of something gray and wet.

I had never before seen one of my own people. I felt like some super-being. Like I was no longer a Yeerk at all. I could see! And in a flash I knew that this one sense was more powerful than every other sense combined. Sight plus powerful limbs! It was inconceivable.

And then my time was up.

I had to leave the Gedd host and return to the pool.

Afterward I communicated with my friends and siblings. Many of them found the whole experience terrifying. Sickening. Awful.

Not me. From that moment on, I swore that I would do whatever it took, pay any price, to have eyes again.

There were more than a quarter million of us on the two transport ships. A quarter million of us and so few hosts. Only the most fit, the most useful, would be given hosts. I would be the most fit. I would be the most useful.

The ship we were in was one we had taken from the Andalites some years earlier. We were using it to travel the galaxy in search of suitable hosts.

Most Yeerks were not interested in the ship. Not even interested in the link we'd managed to create that allowed us to access the Andalite ship's central computer. A computer is a machine made of manipulated matter that stores information, like a flawless memory.

Those who cared about the computer were the scientists and technicians. They learned all they could about Andalite science.

I would never be a scientist. I knew I didn't have that kind of mind. But perhaps there was something else I could learn from the Andalite computer. Something that would make me fit for a host.

I searched the data banks hungrily. And one day I realized I'd found my true calling.

I came across an old Andalite saying in the computer files. <Know your friends well. Know your enemies better.>

The Andalites were our enemies now.

Yes. Know your enemy.

That was my calling. *That* was the way to gaining my own host. I would learn all the computer held about the magnificent, powerful creatures called Andalites.

Someday we would face the Andalites in battle. Then I would be needed.

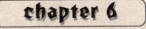

ALDREA

<How are you getting along with your young friend?> my father asked as we galloped across the grass together, side by side.

<Dak? Oh, fine,> I said.

<I notice that you are not making regular data entries. You did for the first three months. Then you stopped.>

I shrugged. <I . . . fell out of the habit, Father.>

<Well, I understand that Dak is almost a friend to you, Aldrea, but we have a mission here. We are supposed to be learning about the Hork-Bajir.>

Actually, Father, I thought privately, *we are supposed to be watching out for any possible Yeerk interest in this planet.* I didn't say that, of course. My father chose to pretend this was some kind of scientific mission. Even now he didn't want to accept the fact that the Yeerks were marauding around the galaxy.

He still preferred to think it was just the Yeerks

33

who had stolen the ships who were guilty. He clung to the belief that the main population of Yeerks were in favor of peace with Andalites.

We would get transmissions from the home world. News that the Yeerks had attacked a moon colonized by Skrit Na and taken additional ships and weapons.

News that the Yeerks had attacked and seized a Hawjabran colony ship. They had attempted to infest the Hawjabrans, but had failed because Hawjabran brains are not centralized, but spread in small nodes throughout their bodies. They had left the Hawjabrans to die. Their ship's life support had been knocked out in the attack. An Andalite courier had come across the ship, drifting, with eight thousand Hawjabrans frozen in the vacuum of space.

News that a group of Ongachic minstrels had been taken and successfully infested. Fortunately for the Ongachic race, they'd long ago abandoned their planet. They are entirely a nomadic, space-faring race now. The Yeerks would have to hunt down literally millions of Ongachic ships spread in every direction through the galaxy. The Ongachic race would survive.

But, my father kept insisting, the Yeerks on their home world have been peaceful, these years since the attack that destroyed his honor.

I didn't point out that the Yeerks on the home

world had no choice: An Andalite fleet was parked in orbit above them, ready to shred anything that tried to come or go in the system.

<I am learning about the Hork-Bajir,> I said. <But I feel like a spy or something, transcribing it all into the computer.>

My father turned his nearest stalk eye toward me and made a small smile. <I'm proud that you wish to keep Dak Hamee's trust,> he said. <But after all, he is Hork-Bajir, not Andalite. I don't think they would even understand the concept of trust, or of "spying," as you call it.>

<Dak understands more than you might think,> I said. *More every day,* I added silently.

We turned and headed back toward the scoop. It was uphill heading back. I ran slowly enough for my father to keep up.

<The Hork-Bajir I've encountered barely function at the level of a small child,> my father said sadly. <The Yeerks were so fascinating. Highly intelligent, yet so limited physically. It's as if the Hork-Bajir are the exact opposite: physically impressive. Mentally . . . well, simple.>

<I think Dak Hamee is different,> I said. <He can read now, and write. And he can do basic math. He's up to calculus. I think he may be capable of n-dimensional geometry.>

My father frowned. <Your mother has studied

the intellectual capacity of Hork-Bajir. I assure you, they are not capable of reading. Not more than recognizing one or two words. And certainly no math beyond what they need to keep track of family members.>

I sighed. I'd been through this before. My parents both assumed I was just exaggerating. Barafin believed me, but he didn't care. Barafin was becoming depressed by the Hork-Bajir planet. There were no other Andalites to recreate with. And of course, Andalites cannot climb trees.

Barafin spent his days near the scoop, playing combat games with the computer.

My father wasn't much better. He'd given up trying to communicate with the Hork-Bajir. They simply had nothing to say that interested him.

My mother was happier, of course. She would go off and study the different trees and the various other animal species.

With my father withdrawn, my mother busy, my brother depressed and indifferent, I was left to myself. So I spent time with Dak. And we explored the valley together.

I had learned to walk on a slant, coping with the slope of the valley. But Dak, like all Hork-Bajir, spent most of his time in the trees. Hork-Bajir are able to run out on branches and leap through the air to the next tree. It's as fast as running along the ground, and easier, when the ground is always at a slant.

One day we were going along this way, me on the ground, my muscles aching from coping with the slope, and Dak leaping easily through the trees, when I saw it.

<Dak! What is that animal?>

"The small, feathered one? It's called a *chadoo*."

It was no more than two feet long and covered in deep blue feathers. It had four short legs and two elongated arms ending in claws. It moved by racing along branches and then leaping through the air, much as Dak did. But the *chadoo* had skin flaps that caught the air like an airfoil, so that it could glide.

"Would you like me to bring it to you, Aldrea?"

I hesitated. What I was thinking of doing was wrong. My parents would be furious if they found out.

If they found out.

<Yes, can you catch it?>

"Of course," Dak said with a laugh. He used his wrist blade to make a horizontal slash in the tree bark. A pale, green-yellow liquid oozed from the gash. He collected some of this on his claw-tip, and held it out to the *chadoo*.

The little blue creature came running. Dak gathered it up carefully and dropped the twenty feet to the ground.

"Here it is," he said, holding it out toward me.

<Dak, do you understand the idea of a "secret"?>

"I have learned very much from you, Aldrea. But I have not learned this."

<A secret is something you know that you never tell anyone else. So that if I tell you something, only you and I will ever know it.>

He looked troubled. "What is the purpose?"

I sighed. Dak had come an amazing way in a very short time. His ability to speak was incredibly improved, for example. And he now fully understood the concept of planets, stars, and galaxies. But he was still Hork-Bajir. And I was still Andalite.

<Trust me,> I said. <And never tell *anyone* what you are about to see.>

I placed my hand on the *chadoo*. And I began to acquire the animal's DNA.

chapter 7

ALDREA

<I am going to change now,> I said. <It may seem frightening. But it isn't magic. It is a new technology we have developed.>

"Technology. Science. Spacecraft and computers," Dak said.

<Yes, like all those things. But different, too. My parents don't even know I have this technology. They don't know that I've used the Escafil Device.>

"This is a secret," Dak said.

<Yes. Dak . . . I am going to become a *chadoo*.>

He had no answer to that. I wasn't surprised. The morphing technology is so new that there are even Andalites who doubt its safety or usefulness. Fortunately, I had a friend back on the home world whose mother was one of the designers of the Escafil Device. She had shown it to me. I'd used it.

<Just don't be afraid. Trust me.>

I began to morph the *chadoo*. It was only the

second time I'd morphed. So as much as I was telling Dak not to be afraid, I was telling myself, too.

I began to shrink. My legs grew shorter, more stunted. My belly sagged toward the ground. My tail seemed to simply wither, as if it were very old and dead and drying up at hyperspeed.

Dak jumped back, eyes wide.

<Don't be afraid,> I told us both. <It won't take long.>

My stalk eyes darkened and disappeared. An opening formed like a cut or sore in the front of my face. Tiny, red teeth sprouted.

My fur grew shaggier, longer. Hundreds of individual hairs twined together to form feathers.

I was on the ground now. My legs were stumps. My arms had grown stronger and longer, relative to the rest of my body. Skin flaps extended down my sides, stretched between back leg and foreleg.

I was no longer Andalite. I was a *chadoo*.

I looked out through *chadoo* eyes. Just two, and only able to see in one direction. It made me feel blind. But they were good eyes, despite there being only two. They saw brilliant color and even more brilliant lines and shapes.

They were eyes adapted for spotting handholds while gliding through the air.

I found the mouth the strangest thing. It felt so

wrong, having this gaping hole in the front of my face. It's silly, but I felt like it was a wound.

The *chadoo's* brain and instincts were gentle enough. This was not an environment with predators. The *chadoo* was almost tame.

<It's still me, Dak,> I said.

"You have become a *chadoo*," he said.

<Yes, but my mind is still the same. I'm still Aldrea. And in a little while, I will change back. But first, I want to know what it's like in your world, up in the trees.>

I had seen some of the valley from the ever-slanted ground. But now I saw the true Hork-Bajir world.

I raced for the trunk of the nearest tree. My four stubby legs each ended in a sharp little claw, and these claws propelled me up the trunk at a shocking speed. Small as I was, and as large as the tree was, the rough bark looked more like a desert plain from the Untouched Wilds on my own world.

I was moving vertically, straight up. I saw an endless expanse ahead of me. To my left and right I saw what might have been the curvature of a small moon or asteroid. The vertical surface curved away, out of sight.

Far ahead of me — upward, that is — I saw what seemed like an entire new tree. It was a

41

branch perpendicular to me. Massive. Huge. Surging up out of the gently curved bark plain.

Dak Hamee kept pace, just behind me. When I paused to look back I became aware of how high up I was. How I was hanging from a vertical surface. If I had let go, I'd have fallen straight down onto Dak.

I paused at the base of the branch. Perspective was bizarre. Up was forward. Down was back. Left and right were emptiness.

"You are really Aldrea?"

<Yes, Dak.>

"Then, come. I will show you my world."

We raced up the tree with Dak in the lead. A hundred feet, two hundred feet, three hundred feet. The valley wall was a hundred feet away now, but always still there.

Higher and higher we went, and yet there remained this bizarre fact that the ground was not so much below us as it was beside us. In the other direction, however, away from the valley wall, there were only trees.

"Follow me!" Dak cried. He swung easily from the trunk onto a massive branch that grew toward the valley center.

My little *chadoo* legs scrabbled to keep up. I raced along the branch. Now I was far, far above the ground, because while it sloped up behind us, it sloped down before us. With each few dozen steps along the branch, I was another ten feet above the ground.

I was beginning to get a glimpse past the trees out into clear air. But we had only begun our wild climb.

We reached the end of the branch. It was so narrow now that I had to hold on by wrapping my stubby legs around and beneath the branch.

"See that treetop?" Dak asked, pointing. "We go that way."

<How?>

"You are a *chadoo,* yes? The *chadoo* knows."

And with that, Dak squatted low, coiling his powerful leg muscles, and leaped into space. He bounced the branch. Down ten feet, up ten, down twenty feet, up twenty, down thirty and up . . . at the top of the arc, he leaped!

He soared and fell, and with a wild grab of his right claw, snagged the top of the next tree.

One claw-hand wrapped around the crown of the tree, and he swung around it, not once, but twice, three times, four times! The crown bent way over from his weight, but it did not break.

It was the most thrilling thing I'd seen before or since. The wild glee of the young Hork-Bajir, swinging madly, five hundred feet above the sloping ground. Swinging and laughing, and then, my hearts — I mean my heart, because the *chadoo* only has one — stopped.

Dak released and fell from sight!

I raced to the end of the branch, trusting the *chadoo* to know what to do. It did. I ran, simply ran, no jumping, no leaping, straight off the end of the branch. Ran straight into the air.

My four feet pushed out, stretching the skin flaps. I felt the wind beneath me, felt it ruffle up into my feathers, felt it fill the skin flaps.

I had lift! I was not merely falling. I could turn my blunt head and change direction. I could raise or lower a leg and change direction even more quickly. I glided along a curved path toward the treetop that still quivered from snapping back.

My thin, strong arms reached and grabbed the tree crown. I swung once around, and down below me, on yet another tree branch, I saw Dak. He was looking up and grinning — a thing Hork-Bajir do with their mouths.

I released and glided down to him.

From then on it was a game. Dak led the way and I followed. A wild, insane romp, leaping across the void, snatching branches from midair, scampering, leaping again.

But always Dak led the way. Tree to tree, along a path he knew as well as I know my own meadow back on the home world.

The trees were changing. The bark became thicker, the treetops higher and higher. At last we reached a tree that made every other tree look like a bush.

From the base of its downhill side to the crown, it was two thousand, one hundred and nineteen feet high. My mother measured it for me days later. I didn't tell her why.

It was almost half a mile tall.

"That is the Tribe Tree," Dak said. "The tree of my people. That is where the elders meet."

I peered at the tree and could see, here and there, platforms, hundreds, thousands of feet up. There were Hork-Bajir there, milling around. The more I looked, the more platforms I saw and the more elaborate they were. Up and up, far over our heads, the platforms twined around the Tribe Tree.

There were hundreds of Hork-Bajir in the tree. Not stripping the bark, but stacking bark carried in by a steady stream of Hork-Bajir.

"Come," Dak said. We raced and leaped and soon I was clinging to the bark of the Tribe Tree itself. Clinging and climbing. Up and up.

<Remember, don't tell your fellow Hork-Bajir who and what I am,> I said.

"They would not understand if I told them," Dak said simply.

We climbed forever. We climbed till I could not imagine that there was still more tree above us. We passed platforms where Hork-Bajir ground up bark. Where they cut bark into strips. Where they bundled bark with string-vines.

And there were other platforms where Hork-Bajir simply sat and seemed to be telling stories. Almost like classrooms, I realized.

Slowly we emerged from the surrounding trees. We climbed till I could see clearly out over the void, across to the far side of the valley. We climbed till I could glimpse the lip of the valley behind us.

Down below, what seemed a million miles below, I saw the toxic blue at the very bottom of the valley. What the Hork-Bajir call "Father Deep."

There was a narrow platform built at the very top of the Tribe Tree. I went up onto it.

<I've been in morph for a long time,> I said. <I have to change back for a while.>

I began to demorph. And a few minutes later, I stood on my own four hooves where no Andalite could ever possibly belong.

With my own proper Andalite eyes I could see in every direction at once. I saw the sheer valley wall behind, the endless trees spreading left and right, the far side of the valley, many miles away. The sky, not as red and gold as it should have been, spread above us, dwarfing the valley. And down below, so far down that I felt nauseated by the drop, I saw a slice of the terrifying "Deep."

I don't know why, but the Deep drew my gaze, even more than the stunning, magnificent vista all around me.

I looked down at the Deep. I looked away and then back down. Near the edge, the trees disappeared, replaced by eerily colored plants in twisted shapes.

<Dak. What is in the Deep?>

He looked at me as if I'd been reading his mind. "I don't know," he admitted. "I only know what my people say."

<What do your people say is in the Deep?>

"Terror," he said simply. "They say that terror is in the Deep."

chapter 8

ESPLIN 9466

It didn't take long for me to become the reigning expert on Andalites. No one else cared. But I was fascinated.

I had "seen" only for a few moments through the Gedd's eyes. But I could try to imagine the life of a four-eyed Andalite. I had to stretch my imagination to picture what it was like to run. To live most of your life directly under the sun and the stars, with only a transparent atmosphere to protect you.

How can a Yeerk, used to the warm intimacy of the Yeerk pool, truly understand what it is like to have four legs, to run, to see, to feel, to manipulate objects at will with delicate, precise hands? To have a deadly tail?

It's not possible. Not really. But I came closer to understanding than anyone else in the pool. I inserted my palps into the computer interface and I read with virtual eyes. And I used that computer simulation of sight to watch, again and again, every stored visual image, still or moving.

Slowly, slowly, I began to understand my enemy. To understand their impressive strengths. But also to see their weaknesses.

The Andalites might have been the dominant species in this arm of the galaxy. But they were not invincible.

Months went by, and slowly the memory of those few amazing moments in the Gedd faded. Others were called to assume hosts. I was not.

But then it happened. Palp to palp, the message came to me. Esplin 9466 to the infestation pier! There was a new species to try. After failures with the Hawjabrans and only the few Ongachics, our wandering assemblage of spacecraft had found a new planet. With new creatures.

Three had been seized from the surface and brought aboard. One was for me.

I was not briefed. I was not given any explanation. I was simply to swim to the infestation pier and wait.

I waited, desperate to control my own excitement. A host! Any host, so long as it had eyes!

Suddenly, I felt the splash as the head was thrust beneath the surface. My senses felt for and found the ear opening. I rushed, afraid that I might fail somehow, afraid this chance would be taken from me.

Instantly I knew this creature was very different from a Gedd. Entry was much easier. The ear canal was large and unobstructed. I released my toxins to numb and dilate the ear, but I wondered if it was even necessary.

I slithered and squeezed till my palps touched the brain. Ah! Very different from the Gedd brain. The brain was divided into lobes, two fairly smooth, one deeply wrinkled. I sank myself into the wrinkles, into the cracks between the lobes. And then I tied in to the brain.

It was not the shock of that first infestation, but it was a revelation!

Hearing was excellent. The sense of smell was almost as good as my own. I opened the eyes.

Ahhh! I cried silently. I had thought the Gedd's vision was all that vision could be. But this creature's eyes were wonderful. The colors so vivid. The lines so clear. I could see depth with amazing precision.

I looked around at the room. Once again, I saw the limited, narrow Yeerk pool that was my whole universe. But my eyes were drawn not to the ship around me, but to my new, personal ship: this body.

One thing was instantly apparent: This was no Gedd. This was no Hawjabran or Ongachic. This body reminded me of the Andalite bodies. It would be fast. It would be powerful. It would be . . .

Dangerous.

I opened the creature's memory, looking for its own pictures of its life. I wanted to know what it could do.

I felt a resistance. A mind within the brain. Stronger than the tired, beaten Gedd. This creature was attempting to fight me!

There was only one possible response.

Total and complete control.

Get out! Get out! the creature screamed in silence.

<Scream all you like,> I sneered. <You belong to me now.>

The creature's mind began to race, searching for some way to stop me. But, of course, there was none. It threatened. It cried. It begged. I felt its desperation, its panic, its fear. And I laughed at the feeble attempt to throw me off.

<Threaten *me*?> I said, mind to mind. <What will you do? Your body is mine now! Your eyes are mine! Your limbs are mine!>

I was giddy. I was in a state of ecstasy! I could crush this mind with ease. It was sad, almost, how easily I defeated the creature. It was feeble compared to me. It had no power to throw me off. No power to retain control.

51

I opened the creature's memory and looked. At first the images were wild, insane, inexplicable. But then the context became clearer. I used more of the memories to get a better understanding.

I saw the world of the creature through its own eyes. I saw its fellows. Its friends. I saw its life . . .

Stripping bark for food. Leaping through the tall trees. Sitting at night and telling stories handed down from generation to generation.

"Well, Esplin-Nine-Four-Double-Six, rrrr-what do you-rrr think?"

It took a moment for me to make sense of the sounds. I listened to see if I could find the source of the sound. And then, it occurred to me: I could use the sense of sight. I could use sight and sound together to pinpoint the source of the sound.

I looked. I moved my eyes and looked again.

Two Gedds stood nearby. I knew that one was Janath 429, a very old Yeerk, and very wise. The other was Akdor 1154. It was Akdor who had led the uprising against the Andalites.

It was Akdor who had first understood the concept of using a host body to act as a predator. It was Akdor who had personally killed four of the Andalite scum.

Akdor moved his Gedd mouthparts and spoke.

"I rrr-asked rrr-what you think. You study-rrr the

rrr-Andalites. Can this body be rrrrr-used to fight the Andalites?"

It was *Galard*, the new language we had learned from the Ongachic hosts. It is the common intergalactic language. The Yeerk language was impossible to speak with Gedd mouths. Even *Galard* came out distorted.

I lowered my eyes and looked down at the body I now owned. I saw blades in several locations. Blades that were used for stripping the edible bark from trees.

It was all so new. So new to all of us. We didn't know anything about the galaxy then.

But I tried to imagine. I saw an Andalite. I pictured this new creature. I placed them together in my imagination. It was hard. Hard to imagine with sight.

"Yes," I said in a harsh, guttural voice. "These creatures will be our weapons."

Akdor and Janath stared at me.

"Then rrrr-we will take this-rrrr species," Akdor announced. "We will make them ourrrrrs. This rrr-planet is wherrrre we make ourr stand! On this planet rrr-we will build the foundations of a true Yeerrrrk empirrrrre!"

I was there. Do you understand what this moment was, what it meant? I was *there* when Akdor announced the birth of the Yeerk Empire.

"So, what arrre these crrrreatures called?" Janath asked me.

I was surprised. Neither Akdor nor Janath knew the name of the species whose doom they had pronounced.

I searched my new memory, ignoring the pitiful, wailing cries that came from the shadow of the creature himself.

"They call themselves Hork-Bajir, Akdor. Hork-Bajir."

chapter 9

DAK HAMEE

<What is that sound?> Aldrea asked. <I have heard it before. Always at this time of night.>

"It is the Speaking Trees," I said.

It was seven weeks since Aldrea had become a *chadoo* for the first time. Since then she had done it again, more than once. But this night she was Andalite.

I liked it best when she was Andalite. I could not care about a *chadoo*. I did care about Aldrea, the Andalite. She had taught me. She had shown me an entire universe unknown to my people.

I was still greedy for knowledge, but Aldrea had begun to say that I knew all she knew. Was this true? It didn't matter. I needed Aldrea the way the leaves need Mother Sky. There was no one else for me to talk to.

In many ways, I was no longer Hork-Bajir. But when we were together and I looked at her delicate shape, I knew that I was not Andalite, either.

<Your trees have the gift of communication, like Andalite trees?> she asked.

"No," I said, smiling. Aldrea had said that Andalite trees could speak in a way. Guide trees: *Garibahs*. But I was not sure I believed it. Our trees did not speak. "We call it the language of the trees, but it is only what we Hork-Bajir use as our primitive communicators. At night the great sound speaks from across the valley. It is how we speak with our brothers and sisters of the other two tribes in the valley. The sound is made by stretched vines. The vine is soaked in rain. Then it is stretched tight, vertically, between high branches and low branches.

"Three of these vines are strung this way, all in one chosen tree. The tree must be a very old *Nawin* tree, for *Nawin* trees become hollow with age. One vine must be ten times the height of a Hork-Bajir. The second must be seven heights. The smallest five heights.

"Two Hork-Bajir climb out on branches and hold a long, straight sapling. This sapling is drawn across the vine, creating a deep sound."

<Resonance,> Aldrea said. <It's almost a type of music.>

"Yes. Sad music tonight," I said. "It is the southern tribe. They tell us that three of their people have been taken to Father Deep."

I listened some more to the low, long, sad notes that vibrated around the valley, echoing from the walls.

"They say that Father Deep has created new monsters. They are . . . small. That's strange. The monsters of the Deep are always larger than us. Yet these were small. Two legs . . . long arms . . . yellow eyes."

Suddenly I felt Aldrea's hand grab my arm above the wrist blade. It was not the first time she had touched me. Usually, I enjoyed the fact that she would grab me for balance, or playfully slap me in pretended upset, or take my hand as we watched the sun turn red. But this was different.

<Can you ask them a question?> Aldrea said. Her thought-speak voice was intense.

"Yes. But as you can see, this system is primitive. Not like an Andalite would make."

<Dak, your people have their own strengths,> Aldrea said. <Ask them about these "monsters." Ask them . . . ask them whether these monsters moved in a clumsy, unbalanced way when they walked.>

I hesitated for a moment. My people had accepted that I was a seer. But I was still young. It was not for me to ask those of the Speaking Tree to transmit messages.

But Aldrea seemed determined. Upset. Or as upset as an Andalite ever becomes. They are not an emotional people.

So I turned and cried into the darkness, shouting toward the Speaking Tree. And a moment later, the much louder, closer sound of our own Speaking Tree rang out, a deep, mournful sound that echoed down the valley.

"What is it that you fear, Aldrea?" I asked her.

<I'm not sure,> she said.

"You do not know if your fear is realized, Aldrea," I pointed out. "But you know what your fear is."

Aldrea laughed. <You keep surprising me, Dak. Every day you're sharper, smarter. You learn so quickly! Your use of language, your perception . . . It's incredible. You could enroll in any Andalite academy tomorrow and —>

"Thank you," I interrupted her. "I have learned from you. I have even learned to recognize when someone is trying to avoid answering a question."

Aldrea formed the strange Andalite smile with her eyes. <I deserved that. Since you ask, I will tell you. What I'm afraid of is —>

But just then the answer was coming from the southern tribe.

"They say these monsters walked in a strange way. As if their legs were different sizes," I translated.

58

The smile disappeared from Aldrea's eyes. <They are,> she said. <Their legs *are* different lengths. We never could figure out why they evolved that way.>

"Who are *they*?"

<They're called Gedds,> Aldrea said.

"Are they from another planet, like Andalites?"

<Yes. But the Gedds aren't the problem. The problem is what those Gedds represent.> She turned all her eyes on me. <Dak, you are the seer. You were born, you say, because your people would need you.>

"Yes, I was born a seer because you Andalites were coming. We had need of one who could learn from you."

<I thought it was that, too,> Aldrea said softly. <But we were both wrong. You were not born because of the coming of Andalites. You were born because the Yeerks are here.>

chapter 10

ALDREA

"What are Yeerks?" Dak Hamee asked me.

I sighed. <They are another species. Different from you or me, from Hork-Bajir or Andalite. Hork-Bajir and Andalites both walk freely in the world. We eat bark or grass. The Yeerks are different.>

"Are they predators? You taught me about predators."

Once again, I was shocked. In the course of a few months Dak Hamee had gone from speaking a sort of childish pidgin to speaking as well as I. His grasp of concepts was sure and swift. The gap between him and the other Hork-Bajir was vast and growing every day. The gap between him and any Andalite . . . well, there no longer was an intellectual gap.

<They are not predators, at least not in the usual way. They are parasites. You see, they . . .>

"What? They what?" Dak pressed.

But my brain had just stopped working. Frozen.

And then, quite suddenly, it began to race in sheer panic.

<Oh, no. NO! They're in orbit!> I cried.

"The Yeerks?"

<They're in orbit! This is the time of night when my father beams his report back to the home world. If they're in orbit they might intercept the message!>

I was already running. Flat-out, tail tucked down, laboring, gasping as my muscles screamed from the pain of fighting the ever-present slope.

Dak loped along as fast as he could, but on the ground I was faster than him. I left him behind. With my stalk eye turned back I saw him leap into the trees. He would move better up there, in his natural element.

But Dak was no longer my concern. I had to stop my father from broadcasting! I had to stop that transmission.

I was two miles from the scoop. Two miles of the weird running required on this planet: serpentine, up a few yards, down a few yards, advancing always, but adding twice the distance. It was simply impossible to run any other way. Uphill, downhill, running around the massive trees.

I was extremely upset by the time I came in sight of the lights of the scoop. Upset because I knew in my hearts it was too late. My father has always been very precise. Very punctual. And my internal clock told me that the message had gone out fifteen minutes ago.

Still I ran. I could make out the lights of the scoop. I could see shadows and silhouettes as my father or mother or brother moved in front of the lights. I could imagine every detail. My mother working at her computer, entering a precise DNA analysis of some strange, new flower she'd found. My brother playing a holo game, lancing imaginary enemy ships. My father . . . my father standing quietly on his own, thinking, remembering, imagining. Dreaming his hopeful dreams.

That is the picture I want to hold onto, forever. Not what happened next.

chapter 11

ESPLIN 9466

I had enjoyed two days in my new Hork-Bajir body. It was still a wonder to me. A miracle.

The only unpleasant part was the constant, nagging cries from the Hork-Bajir mind. It wasn't that he refused to accept the new reality. He was simply too stupid to know what was happening. Too stupid to understand.

I walked throughout the ship now. It was built for Andalites, of course, so most of the floor had once been growing, green, red, and blue grass. The ceilings had been wonderful holographic images of an Andalite sky.

Andalites hate confinement. I knew that about them. I knew that they were building a new generation of spacecraft that would be called "Dome ships." These Dome ships would actually have huge, artificial parks. Grass and trees and open sky.

But the grass on this transport had long since

63

died. We had no use for grass. And we have no fear of confinement.

Here and there were yellowed patches that had managed somehow to struggle on, but for the most part the underlying steel mesh was visible.

Visible! The very idea was new to me. That there were things one could see, and other things one could not see.

The Andalite ship was built for transport. But there was a transparent portion of the hull I could look through with my eyes and see the other ships in our little armada.

Nearby, close enough to see, were a pair of Andalite fighters. We had four altogether. Plus the two transports. We had also seized a small Ongachic craft and three Skrit Na ships. The Skrit Na ships were slow but well-armed. The Ongachic ship was faster but carried no weapons.

Down below, filling half my field of vision, was the Hork-Bajir planet. It was the first planet I had ever seen. It was infinitely different from feeling, smelling, listening to descriptions. To see it, hanging there in space . . . it was overwhelming. So huge! So strange.

"Esplin," a voice said. I turned to see another Hork-Bajir host body.

It was Carger 7901. I had known Carger for a

long time. But I had never liked him. There had always been something too crude, too violent about him. Too ambitious. And now Carger was one of my few fellow Hork-Bajir-Controllers.

There was talk of creating new ranks. Everyone said that if we were going to become a conquering army, we would need a hierarchy. The ancient Council of Thirteen would remain all-important. But beneath that would come something called "vissers" and "sub-vissers."

Carger had already begun to refer to himself as a sub-visser. No one had contradicted him.

"Esplin. Come with me."

"Why?"

"Don't ask questions," Carger said. "Just come."

I followed him. He led me toward the docking area just behind the bridge.

There we met up with two Gedd-Controllers I didn't know. And Akdor was there as well.

"Rrr-we have just rrrrreceived an interrrcept coming from the surrrrface below," he said tersely. "An rrr-*Andalite* broadcast."

I felt the surge of hormones within the Hork-Bajir body. The surge that came with fear or the anticipation of action.

"Therrrre is an rrr-Andalite outpost on the planet.

Rrr-the brrrroadcast was not encoded. We believe there arrrre just fourrrr Andalites. They must be rrr-killed. Immediately, before they can discoverrrr ourrrr presence here."

Carger smiled with his Hork-Bajir mouth. "I will be honored to command the attack."

"No doubt you rrr-would," Akdor said tersely. "But you are only going so that rrr-we can put those Hork-Bajirrrr bodies to use. We will attack from the rrr-Andalite fighter crrrraft. But if all four of the Andalites are not killed, you two will go after the survivorrrrs."

I'll admit I felt a qualm at that. Unlike the others, I knew about Andalites. I knew how advanced their technology was, and how dangerous. I also knew that even without any other weapons, with tails alone, they were dangerous.

But I would have died rather than admit those doubts. This was the path to power. To be there, in the first combat use of Hork-Bajir hosts, would be an important thing.

And if Carger could call himself a sub-visser, why shouldn't I be one as well?

Two of the Andalite fighters were brought in to dock with the transport. Carger and I went aboard one.

It was a short ride down to the planet surface.

Half an orbit, then down through the thin atmosphere. The two fighters stayed close together in formation. I had taught our pilots that concept. I had learned it from studying the Andalites. Spacecraft in formation are harder to attack.

Not that we expected to be attacked. There were four Andalites on the planet surface. But no ship.

Down we went, skimming across the surface of the planet. And then, down, down into one of the huge valleys.

It was dark on this side of the planet. Night. Eyes do not function well at night. But it didn't matter. We knew where the Andalites were.

We came in just inches above the treetops.

"Pilot," I said. "My studies of Andalite methods reveal that this ship possesses a visual augmentation device."

The pilot — a Gedd-Controller, of course — snorted like I was a fool. "We know ourrrr ship," he said. He flipped on the viewscreen. And there on the screen, I could see the Andalite dwelling. A "scoop," they call it.

I saw that one Andalite was working at a computer interface. A smaller, younger one seemed to be cavorting, playing some game. I saw a large, probably male Andalite standing at the edge of the scoop, looking out into the darkness.

"Looking the wrong way," Carger laughed. "Look up, Andalite. Look up and see your death!"

The Gedds joined in the laughter. Laughter: the ability to express joy with mouth sounds. So much that was new!

But I did not laugh. "I see three Andalites, not four," I said.

"The fourth is probably inside the scoop," Carger said.

"No. Andalites never take shelter unless they must. In the depth of a cold night, or to avoid harsh weather, or to fend off an attack. Or when they must serve aboard spacecraft. Andalites are creatures of the open spaces. They hate being confined in any way. They become nervous and afraid if they don't have large areas in which to run."

Carger sneered. "You are quite the Andalite-lover, Esplin."

I felt a prickling of the skin on the back of my neck. It is a Hork-Bajir fear reaction. Fear of Carger.

"I will kill more Andalites if I know their habits," I said gruffly.

The two fighters were now no more than three hundred feet above the scoop, engines on very low to avoid being heard or seen. Another tactic I had discovered from my study of the enemy.

"Shredderrrr powered. Tarrrget rrr-acquired," the Gedd pilot said.

"There are only three Andalites in view," I said. "Wait till the fourth one joins them."

"Wait? Fool. Shoot!" Carger demanded.

"No! The remaining Andalite will see the —"

"I said shoot!" Carger roared. "That is a direct order from your sub-visser! Shoot! Kill them now!"

chapter 12

ALDREA

There was no warning. No warning, except for the awful feeling in my stomach, the churning, awful feeling of dread.

TSEEEWWWWW!

TSEEEWWWWW!

The shredder beams fired from the sky. Not too far up. They had come low, snuck closer, and hovered, lights off, hidden by trees and darkness.

TSEEEWWWWW!

TSEEEWWWWW!

The scoop exploded. The air pockets in the construction material superheated in a microsecond and exploded. The moisture in the ground, in the grass and soil turned to steam in half the blink of an eye and exploded. Everything that could burn, burned.

And everything can burn in the heat of a shredder at full power. Everything.

<NOOOOOOO!> I screamed.

I felt the blast of heat on my face. I felt the concussions roll across me like waves.

<NOOOOOO!>

TSEEEWWWWW!

TSEEEWWWWW!

The scoop was all flames and explosion. I didn't see my family burn. I didn't see them, but I knew it was happening.

A hundred feet away, less, they were already dead. Dead with the first shredder blast.

<AAHHH! AAHHH! AAHHH! AAHHH!>

I couldn't stop screaming.

The two stolen Andalite fighters fired. Again and again. Fired till what had been our scoop was nothing but fused glass. Molten slag.

<AAHHH! AAHHH! AAHHH!>

Someone grabbed me. I whipped my tail without thinking, enraged, terrified.

Dak Hamee took the blow on his left arm. My tail blade sliced through half his wrist blade. A small blade piece fell to the ground.

The shredder fire stopped. What had been our scoop, what had been my family, glowed red in the night. It would be days before the heat dissipated.

"You must get away!" Dak said fiercely.

<They're dead,> I moaned. <No, no, no, no.>

"You must get away!" he said again.

<They're all dead!>

"The ones who did this may come to check, to be sure of what they have done," Dak said. "They must not find you."

<What does it matter? Oh, my mother. My father. Barafin! Barafin!>

Dak grabbed me and turned me away from the awful scene. He took my head gently in his two claw hands and made me face him. But as a Hork-Bajir, he didn't understand: My stalk eyes could all too easily stay riveted on the glowing red wound that had been my life.

"As you said, Aldrea, this is why I was born a seer. To save my people from these Yeerks who have done this evil thing. But I cannot do it alone. You must help me."

<Help?> I sobbed. <Help what?>

"Help me to understand . . . to understand this evil," Dak said. "Will you help me understand this evil?"

I was sick. So sick with fear and hatred I wanted to die just to make the sickness stop.

But Dak had shown me a way to live. A reason to endure the violence eating away at my insides.

<No, I won't help you to *understand*,> I said. <But I will help you kill Yeerks. That, I will do. I will

help you kill them. And kill them. And kill them! And kill them all!>

I screamed in powerless rage at the sky where I knew the Yeerks were hiding.

<Kill them all!> I cried. <Kill them all!>

chapter 13

DAK HAMEE

I was still shaking. My face still burned from the awful heat. My mind was reeling, swirling, crazed by what I had seen.

All I knew of Andalites and the galaxy beyond my planet was what Aldrea had told me. She had not told me of such things. She had not told me of weapons. Of wars. Of Yeerks.

I knew none of these things.

I knew that there were monsters who lived in Father Deep and sometimes rose up to take unwary Hork-Bajir who had gone too far down the valley walls.

But those were monsters. They did not use spacecraft. They did not strike, invisibly, from the sky.

I knew this, though: When monsters attack, a Hork-Bajir must run away. If one monster attacks and fails to drag you away, another monster may be drawn by the noise and attack as well. These Yeerks might be like that. They might still attack again.

Aldrea was not listening to me. I took her arm with my hand and pulled her away. I made her follow me into the shadows, away from the horrible glow.

I had to tell the elders of this. Nothing like this had ever happened. They had to know. They would have to decide . . .

No, I realized. I would have to decide. They would look at me and say, "Dak Hamee, you are the different one. You are the seer. Tell us the way."

I stopped running. Aldrea stopped, too.

"I must decide," I said. I felt as though a Tribe Tree had fallen on me. I thought I had learned so much. I thought I was wise. But I knew nothing!

"I'm not ready," I said to Aldrea. "I don't know what to do!"

Before she could answer, I saw two Hork-Bajir coming toward us, running. They must have seen the lights from the sky.

"Do not fear, brothers," I said to them.

"Oh, we're not afraid," one said to me. His tone was strange. Different.

He walked straight toward me. As he drew close, I realized I did not know him. Was he from one of the other tribes in the valley?

Ssslash!

He struck me with his wrist blade! I was cut in my chest. I could see the blood. I could see that the skin was separated, as though a large mouth had been cut into my chest.

It caused pain.

"Why did you —"

Ssslash! Ssslash!

He struck at me, using his feet and elbow blades!

I was cut again. I was bleeding. The left side of my face was deeply gashed. It had all happened in the blink of an eye.

"Forget him, get the Andalite!" the other Hork-Bajir yelled.

The second Hork-Bajir leaped at Aldrea. He was slicing the air with his blades, whirling and slicing, as if doing a sky-dance.

<Dak! Fight back. These aren't real Hork-Bajir!> Aldrea said.

"What?"

<Fight them!> Aldrea yelled, and she swung her tail, whipping it forward so fast that the air cracked. The small blade on the end of her tail struck directly into the chest of the second Hork-Bajir.

He leaped back, hissing furiously.

All I could do was stare. I was bleeding. I was cut in many places. I felt pain. But more, I felt confused. How was it possible for a Hork-Bajir to cut me with his blades? It was not an accident, like sometimes happens when we are harvesting bark.

We were not harvesting bark. This Hork-Bajir had cut me. Deliberately! Why?

"Ignore the stupid one, help me get the Andalite! She cut me!"

Now both Hork-Bajir turned to Aldrea. They moved closer, slashing madly at air, drawing closer all the time. They circled, forcing her back against a tree trunk.

If they kept slashing and moving toward her in that way, she would be cut. She would be cut so badly that she might die. I had seen Hork-Bajir who had been accidentally cut. Once an old, weak Hork-Bajir died from the cut.

Aldrea's tail quivered, poised.

A sudden leap! Both Hork-Bajir jumped at Aldrea, blades flashing. Aldrea's tail whipped again and again.

She tripped! One of her legs buckled and she sagged to one side.

"Die, Andalite filth!" one of the Hork-Bajir screamed.

His blades flashed.

I looked at my own wrist blades.

Aldrea screamed in rage and terror.

I held out my arms and saw the blades there. It was as if I were seeing myself for the first time.

77

Something happened then. It was as if I had been given the power to look right into the heart of Father Deep. I could feel a terrible knowledge, a terrible understanding. I could feel . . . *power*.

<Dak! Help me!>

I jumped on the back of the closest Hork-Bajir. I swung my arm as hard and as fast as I could. My wrist blade sliced into his back. It sliced through the muscle. It sliced through his spine.

Every muscle in his body went limp instantly. He fell back, unable to move his legs.

I leaped at the other Hork-Bajir, but he was backing away, turning, running.

"Carger, you coward!" the crippled Hork-Bajir cried.

I stared at my wrist blade. It dripped with blood.

<Gedds!> Aldrea yelled.

I followed the direction of her main eyes. Two loping, strange, small monsters were approaching. They held small machines in their hands.

<We have to run!> Aldrea said.

"Run?" I was still staring stupidly at my own blades.

The Hork-Bajir at my feet groaned. His arms moved weakly. His legs moved not at all.

Aldrea bent her upper body to bring her face very close to the wounded Hork-Bajir. <Whatever your name is, Yeerk, go tell your masters: First your

treason destroyed my father, and then you murdered him and my entire family. But you will not have this planet. We are the Andalites, you parasite worm. And we'll see you all dead. You and your entire filthy race. Tell your masters that.>

The two creatures Aldrea called Gedds were rushing forward now, raising the small machines in their hands.

<The daughter of Seerow will show you the other side of the Andalite character,> Aldrea said to the crippled Hork-Bajir.

Then Aldrea and I ran.

chapter 14

ALDREA

My family was dead. I was the only Andalite within many millions of miles. I had no way of communicating with my people. The Yeerks had come to the Hork-Bajir world, and only Dak and I knew.

I'd known that the Hork-Bajir were peaceable. I'd had no idea before this that they simply did not understand the very concept of fighting.

They were among the fiercest-looking, most physically awesome, sentient species in the galaxy. They were walking weapons. Deadly from head to foot. But they didn't know it. They didn't know what it meant.

They were perfect targets for the Yeerks.

We ran, easily losing the Gedds. We kept moving, always downhill, not knowing if we ran from real pursuers or merely from phantoms. I tried to figure out what to do. But my mind would not let go of the picture of shredders reducing all I cared about to fused, glowing slag.

"Tell me about these Yeerks," Dak asked me, panting.

That much I could do. <They are a parasitic species. They are able to live on their own in something called a Yeerk pool. But they prefer life inside the body and brain of other species.>

"How is this possible?"

<The Yeerks are as they have evolved. They are parasites by nature. Evolution has equipped them to do this. On their own world they infest a species called Gedds. You saw some Gedds back there. My father was the first Andalite to make real contact with them.>

Dak looked surprised. "You have lived among these Yeerks?"

<Yes. We . . . my father and mother were sent to study them. And to learn if we could make allies of them. Or to learn if we had any reason to fear them.>

Dak nodded. "This is what your parents did here, too. Am I correct? They were sent to study us."

<Yes. But there was a difference. We knew the Yeerks to be highly —> I stopped myself.

Dak waited for a moment. Then he finished my sentence for me. "You knew the Yeerks to be highly intelligent. Unlike Hork-Bajir. You were interested in them for their intelligence. And you feared them for the same reason."

<Yes, Dak. It was their intelligence that interested us.>

"It is why your father and mother had no real interest in us. We are a stupid species."

He sounded bitter. Not at me. Not at Andalites. But at his own people. Like he was ashamed of them.

<Intelligence isn't everything,> I said. <My father is . . . was . . . brilliant. But the Yeerks tricked my father. He taught them about the world beyond their planet. He taught them about written language, about the very concept of manipulating matter, toolmaking, sight, art, everything. He trusted them. He thought they were grateful. He thought they would be content.>

"Your father made a mistake," Dak said. "The Yeerks *were* content. But by showing them all they did not have, they began to want more. They wanted to be like you. Like Andalites."

I turned my stalk eyes to stare at Dak as he trotted beside me. How did he cut so quickly to the heart of the problem? How could he guess how the Yeerks felt?

Of course. Because he felt the same way. He, too, was jealous of what we Andalites had. Jealous of our power, our knowledge, our intelligence.

<The Yeerks slaughtered most of the Andalites with my father,> I said. <They stole Andalite ships.

They escaped into space. Since then they have been looking for suitable host bodies.>

"And now they have found them," Dak Hamee said darkly.

<Yes.>

"My people will be unable to stop them."

<Maybe not,> I said eagerly. <You Hork-Bajir could be very dangerous, very powerful fighters, at least in close combat. One-on-one you could even challenge an Andalite warrior.>

Dak laughed. "My people do not understand 'parasites.' They will never understand that these creatures will steal their bodies. They will listen to what we tell them, then they will go on with stripping bark and playing and caring for their children."

<Maybe not. You are the seer. You were born to teach your people a new thing. Maybe you were born to teach your people to fight. Maybe your purpose is to teach Hork-Bajir to kill Yeerks.>

"I hoped I had been chosen to show my people all the things your father tried to show the Yeerks. I wanted to teach them music. Writing. Art. I wanted to teach them to keep track of time, the passing of years. To make tools, to build. But your father gave those things to the Yeerks, and now we see the results. Maybe I was a fool to think that knowledge would make my people happy."

<There will be time to think about all that after

83

we find a way to annihilate the Yeerks,> I said. <We can save your people, if they will learn to fight! They don't have to be destroyed.>

"Yes, they do," he said quietly. "Either they will learn to fight and hurt and kill, or they will learn to be slaves. Both will destroy them. Killers or slaves. They will be one or the other. Killers or slaves."

I stopped and grabbed Dak Hamee's arm. I deliberately moved my fingers down to the blade at his elbow. It was almost as hard as an Andalite male's tail blade. And just as sharp.

<If the choice is between being a killer and being a slave, be a killer. You did it back there. It isn't so hard to learn.>

"And that's what you want for me? To be a killer?"

<If necessary, yes!>

Dak slowly removed my hand from his blade. He was careful not to cut me.

I met his gaze. Hork-Bajir are not good at concealing their feelings. They've never tried to learn the art of lying. So I could see what was in Dak's mind and heart.

"There is much I still have to learn about Andalites," he said.

I looked away. It is hard seeing disappointment in the eyes of someone you care for. And yet, his contempt for me changed nothing. He had no choice. His people had no choice. Would I help make them a race of killers in order to stop the Yeerks? Yes. A thousand times over, yes.

The creatures who had murdered my family would pay. No matter what.

TSEEEWWW!

The tree trunk just inches to my left exploded! Splinters struck me, cut me. The concussion and light stunned me.

But it was a handheld shredder, not one of the high-powered weapons from the fighters. I caught a glimpse of Gedds loping toward us, closing in from two sides.

Somehow they had tracked us. And more had been brought down from the orbiting ships.

They were above us uphill. The only way to run was downhill.

<They've found us!> I cried. <Run!>

We ran. We were faster than the Gedds, but I knew they would call in the fighters. And we could not outrun the fighters.

TSEEEWWW! TSEEEWWW!

"We must go to Father Deep," Dak said.

<Can we survive down there?>

"Can we survive *here*?"

We raced down the valley, down and down toward the glowing, blue mist the Hork-Bajir called Father Deep.

chapter 15

ALDREA

Down, down, always downhill. My leg muscles screamed in pain. I wanted to stop and morph into the *chadoo*. But there was no time. The Gedds were coming. And I could hear them talking on their communicators, trying to bring the fighters in for the kill.

We were being saved by the topography of the planet. The Yeerk fighter pilots seemed confused. They didn't know whether they should position themselves above us or straight out from us. It was a problem an Andalite would have easily solved. But the Yeerks were still new to the entire world of sight. The trees, the sharp slope baffled them.

But not for long.

TSEEEEWWWWW!

A two-foot-wide hole burned straight through the trunk of a tree just ahead of us. The hole smoked but the tree trunk did not explode.

TSEEEWWWW!

A shredder beam ripped a trench in the ground beside us.

Still we ran. A nightmare of terror. Pain in every cell of my body. Wounds oozing blood. Muscles desperate for rest.

Down and down and down. And now through the trees I could catch glimpses of the glowing blue. Already the air was thicker.

How many miles had we run? I was running at full speed, heedless of obstacle. Panic speed. Terror speed.

Ahead of us, a knot of five or six scared Hork-Bajir. They huddled together, watching the sky, watching the shredder fire, grotesque faces made even more grotesque by fear.

"It's Dak Hamee!" one cried. "Dak Hamee! Seer! What is happening?"

"Run! Run away!" Dak cried.

TSEEEWWWW!

Shredders reduced two of the Hork-Bajir to vapor. A third was hit by the edge of the beam. He lived long enough to see that his legs, his body below the waist, was gone.

"Run away! Tell everyone to hide!" Dak screamed. "I have to help them, show them!" he said to me.

<It's us the Yeerks want,> I said. <If we stay with these people they'll be in greater danger.>

Even as I said the words I knew I had lied. It wasn't *us* the Yeerks were chasing. It was me. All Hork-Bajir were the same to the Yeerks. It was the Andalite they wanted to kill.

But Dak accepted my warning. He followed me down the hill, leaving behind the terrified Hork-Bajir.

No time for guilt. I had to survive! Only I could reach my people and bring them to annihilate the Yeerks. Only I could ensure vengeance. What were a few scared Hork-Bajir compared to the need to kill the Yeerks?

The air was thicker still. It was like breathing cold steam. But the extra oxygen renewed my strength.

Suddenly, there it was below us. The trees were gone. The ground was open. Swirling, blue mist glowed dangerously.

But right then my choice was not between a long and happy life on the one hand and death on the other.

My choice was to live for a few minutes more or die right then. I chose to take the few minutes.

I plunged into Father Deep.

chapter 16

DAK HAMEE

We have many tales, we Hork-Bajir, of Father Deep. Father Deep and Mother Sky gave birth to us, their children. Mother Sky gives us air and light. Father Deep gives us soil and water. Both are necessary for the trees that sustain us.

But Father Deep is also the place from which monsters come.

No Hork-Bajir has ever entered Father Deep and lived to tell of it.

Now we were entering the Deep. We had passed the zone of bright bushes and distorted flowers at the edge of the Deep. No trees grew here. But things still lived, even now, with the blue mist all around us, concealing us from our pursuers.

<This atmosphere appears to be breathable,> Aldrea said. <I don't know the precise ratio of gases, of course, but I am able to breathe. And you, Dak?>

"Yes. I can breathe." My voice sounded flat. It

seemed to die in the air. As though the sounds could not possibly get from my mouth to Aldrea's ears.

I was frightened. I knew we would die. But I also knew that it was better to die here in Father Deep than to be killed by the Yeerks.

Father Deep was ours. Of our world. Of the Hork-Bajir. I would die like a Hork-Bajir.

The world around us became a deeper blue. Light seemed to come from below us, glowing all around us. It was a blue fog. Thicker and thicker, till I could barely see Aldrea though she was only a few heights away.

I waited for the monsters to leap out and seize me. My skin tingled, awaiting the deadly touch. But nothing came.

<The temperature is rising as we descend,> Aldrea said.

I realized I was walking on lush, thick grass. As we descended ever farther, the fog seemed to be thickening. Aldrea was no more than a blue shadow within blue mist.

I'd heard nothing of our pursuers. Not a sound since we'd entered the Deep. Had they been frightened off?

Beside me, a shape emerging. A monster?

"Aldrea?" I said, my voice quavering.

Closer, closer . . . a Gedd!

TSEEEEWWWW!

A flash of light. Not the beam I'd seen before, but something like a ball of lightning.

"Rrrr-aaarrrgghh!" the Gedd screamed.

A touch on my arm.

I leaped and spun around.

<It's me,> Aldrea said.

"Rrr-aaarrr arrrgghh!" the Gedd cried.

<This atmosphere is too dense for a shredder,> Aldrea said. <It's a weapon designed for a vacuum, or at least for a decently clear atmosphere. He got flashback. Shredder energy absorbed by the atmosphere and reflected.>

The Gedd continued screaming, but his voice was deadened by the mist as we went down, ever down, into the Deep.

Suddenly, I felt a tear in the mist, a breath of wind. For just a moment I could clearly see a pair of Gedds standing ahead of us! Their shredders were aimed. And now, looming up beside them, I saw the Hork-Bajir who had attacked us before. The one who had run away.

"Don't fire those shredders, you fools," the Hork-Bajir ordered. "Can't you hear Arklan screaming?"

<Two Gedds and you, Hork-Bajir-Controller, against the two of us?> Aldrea laughed. <Without your shredders, you don't have the guts.>

The Hork-Bajir nodded. "The shredders will be

safe enough up close." To the Gedds he said, "Wait till we are within five feet, then fire!"

The three of them ran straight at us. Aldrea dodged left. I dodged right.

WHUMPF!

I slammed into something that cried out, "Rrrrrrr!"

A Gedd! I was on the ground. The Gedd was beside me. Then, in a flash, the creature Aldrea had called a Hork-Bajir-Controller was standing over me. He drew his own shredder and pressed the end of it against my head.

I could see the mad glee in his eyes. I could see his finger tightening on the trigger.

And then . . .

The Hork-Bajir was yanked straight up off the ground. Up into the air, as if he'd been launched by a bent branch. He flew up, then stopped.

I saw the two massive, three-fingered hands of the *Jubba-Jubba* close around the Hork-Bajir's chest. I heard a cry. A roar. And the Hork-Bajir's body fell to the ground on top of me.

A body with no head.

"Aaaahhhh!" I cried in terror.

The Gedd beside me rolled to his feet and began to run. A three-fingered hand reached down out of the mist and snatched the Gedd up.

No part of the Gedd fell back to the ground. No

part of his body, at least. The shredder clattered a few feet from me.

In panic I got up on my hands and knees and crawled to the weapon. I grabbed it in my hands. My clumsy fingers fumbled with the unfamiliar device. My too-large fingers found the trigger. I aimed it upward.

The three-fingered hand came down, down, down toward me.

I aimed the shredder.

FWAPP!

It was too fast to see! The mist swirled, revealing where the lightning movement had come from.

FWAPP! FWAPP!

Aldrea's tail flashed again and again, and there came a roaring howl like nothing I had ever heard or imagined. A huge, three-fingered hand fell to the ground.

Fell and lay there. Dead. Severed from the monster.

The monster screamed in rage.

<Get up! We must run!> Aldrea cried.

I got up. I moved. I dropped the shredder, not wanting to hold it any more.

The *Jubba-Jubba* monster did not follow. For the first time in history, a monster of Father Deep had been defeated.

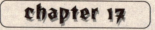

ALDREA

Dak looked at me like I was some sort of mythological deity. I had injured the monster. I guess no one had even done that before.

But it had been a close thing. I hated to admit it, but a big, male Andalite warrior could have done it with a single tail strike. It took me three.

And yet I had done it.

I felt satisfaction, no more. My war was not against these monsters, as Dak called them. My war was with the Yeerks.

"We should get away before more monsters come," Dak said.

<No. By now the entire area back up there above the mist will be crawling with Yeerks. They can't afford to let me live. They can't let *either* of us live,> I added hastily. <They'll bring down all the Gedds they have, and all the Hork-Bajir, too, if they have more of them.>

"Then we must stay within the Deep," Dak said

grimly. "We must stay here in the realm of monsters, while my people are taken by these Yeerks."

<Maybe your people will fight.>

"No. They will be taken. They will be made into slaves of the Yeerks. They will not fight. I might have saved them. Instead I followed you, Aldrea."

I didn't know if he was angry at me, or angry at himself. Both, I guessed. Would he leave me? No. He cared for me. We had more in common than he could ever have with any Hork-Bajir. It was too late for Dak: He knew that the stars were not flowers.

And having learned so much, he still needed to learn more. He was hungry for it, for ideas, for knowledge, for skills. And only I could feed that hunger.

No, he would stand by me, I was sure of that. He would hate himself for making that choice. But that didn't matter, not now. All that mattered now was destroying the Yeerks.

<Dak, eventually, we must find a way to contact my people,> I said. <We may have to steal a Yeerk ship. We may have to fly, Dak. We may have to go up into space.>

It was what Dak wanted most, I knew. To experience space. To fly up to the stars. It was a promise he could never refuse. A bribe.

Dak stopped walking. I stopped and turned back to face him. <What's the matter?>

"You did not have to say that, Aldrea. You do not have to hold out a ripe *Nawin* cone to make me stay with you. All this time together, Aldrea, and yet you don't know that I would sacrifice anything for you?"

I could only stare. Stare and burn with humiliation. He had seen right through me. I felt small and shabby. I should have said I was sorry. But that, too, would have been a lie.

You see, at that moment, nothing mattered to me. Nothing but erasing the pain of watching my family burn. What Dak thought of me, even what I thought of myself: None of that really mattered.

Dak would stay with me. And I would find a way to pay the Yeerks back.

<Dak, do you have any idea what is farther down in the Deep?>

"No, Aldrea. Already we have gone farther than any Hork-Bajir ever."

<Let's go farther still,> I said. There was no other option.

We walked more slowly now, always downhill. It was a nervous walk. The mist was all around us. We had seen one of the monsters already, and I now knew they were not mere myth.

But I was pretty sure we had lost any Yeerk pursuit. At least for the moment.

And yet, although we Andalites are not superstitious, we do have our own ancient myths of dark, deep places within the ground. Places of fear and loathing. And those myths were surfacing in my mind now.

"The mist grows thinner," Dak said.

He was right. I could see him more clearly. And now I was beginning to be able to see down the slope a short distance. Nothing but scruffy, blazingly red and green and blue bushes. No monsters. Not that I could see, anyway.

Down and down we went. Hour after hour. Down, ever down, through a weird twilight. Without being attacked. Without seeing any more monsters. Had our small victory scared them off?

I swiveled my stalk eyes constantly. And then I happened to look up. The sky was brilliant blue.

<It's some kind of vapor barrier,> I said. <Some­how the atmosphere down here in the Deep inter­acts with the atmosphere in the valley above us and forms a layer of vapor. The blue color must be a by-product of the interaction.>

I tried to run through my basic chemistry and get some idea what we were breathing. I came up with some possibilities. None of them exactly comforting. Still, the air, while horribly humid and thick, was breathable.

"Down here one cannot even see the valley above," Dak said. "A creature living here would think the blue mist was the sky."

He was right. Only the source of light was below us, not truly above. I knew that beyond the blue barrier it was night. And yet the blue glowed, reflecting light.

As we went ever downward, the light brightened. It was still a sickly, unnatural light. More radioactive than radiating, if you know what I mean. But at least we could see.

And what we saw was that the landscape around us was home to a bizarre array of the brightly colored bushes and a few stunted, twisted trees that Dak refused to acknowledge were trees at all. Here and there, absurdly fast streams cut through the sparse, tired grass and into the bare rock underfoot. You could hear the water racing, having gathered momentum all the way down from the valley above. Some streams were quite large, eight or ten or fifteen feet across.

We began to realize that the ground was leveling off just a little. It was almost as flat as the meadow where we'd built our scoop. Flat, by Hork-Bajir standards.

But the land seemed to stop or fall away, less than a quarter mile ahead.

We advanced cautiously, slowly. And then, quite

suddenly, we could see the end of the land. It simply stopped.

"What can this be?" Dak asked.

<I don't know,> I admitted. <It's *your* planet.>

"Not this part of it."

Step by step, closer, closer. Till we stood on the very edge of the cliff. I arched my upper body forward. I could not imagine how Dak could deal with the height, standing on only two legs with nothing but a tail to help support him.

I looked down, fearful.

Then I looked down again in utter astonishment.

It was a chasm. Sheer cliffs on both sides. Sheer as walls. I could see across the chasm to the far side far better than I could see straight down.

The walls of the chasm were covered in an amazing, intricate filigree: windows, doors, walkways, arches, open spaces cut back into the cliff. All connected vertically by stone stairways.

Thousands of feet below, below all this incredible construction, maybe tens of thousands of feet, was the valley floor. It was not as bright as a sun. But it was bright enough to cast shadows upward from every stair and arch and windowsill.

It glowed red and yellow and seemed to seethe with slow, sluggish movement.

We were looking at the molten heart of the planet.

chapter 18

ESPLIN 9466

In an instant I had learned one of the terrible drawbacks of having a host body. A host body can be hurt. And the pain cannot be filtered out. The very capability that gives us control ties us into the pain.

The Hork-Bajir had slashed me with his blade. He had aimed the blow well. The spine of my host body was cut in two. All of the body below my chest ceased to exist.

I lay helpless. No one came. For a very long time I lay there, staring up at the night sky through the ominous Hork-Bajir trees.

I saw spacecraft landing. I heard the grunts of Gedds, rushing around in futile pursuit of the Andalite.

Only hours later did anyone come looking for me.

They dragged me aboard the nearest fighter and

100

ferried me back up to the transport ship. I drained back into the Yeerk pool. I was blind again.

Blind, and being interrogated mercilessly.

<Where did the Andalite girl go?>

<I don't know.>

<How many Hork-Bajir were with her?>

<Only one.>

<What happened to Carger?>

<He ran away. Beyond that, I don't know.>

Over and over again. And the more I was questioned, the more I learned. A total of seven of our people had passed through the blue vapor barrier. One had survived to tell wild tales of huge, shambling monsters appearing out of the mist.

Eventually it was decided that the Andalite girl must have died, too. If these monsters had killed our people, surely they had killed the Andalite as well.

Only I disagreed. <Just because some Gedds were killed, just because Carger was killed, that does not mean the Andalite died.>

<Do you mean to imply that an Andalite girl is stronger, braver, more resourceful than our own warriors?>

<Yes,> I said. <Yes. The Andalites did not become the dominant species in this part of the galaxy by being weak or stupid or cowardly.>

But no one listened. And I was left to wander,

blind, around the home that had once been my entire universe and was now a filthy trap.

At last, days later, when enough Hork-Bajir had been taken, I was given a new host body. A new Hork-Bajir.

"We have sent strong, armed parties into the blue mist," Akdor told me. He now had a Hork-Bajir host body, too. "The monsters are real. They have killed more of us. We found the bodies of the others. We searched for the body of the Andalite, but did not find it."

I listened, trying not to gloat too openly.

"It seems you were right, Esplin-Nine-Four-Double-Six. Now you will go back to the surface. You will find this Andalite. You will destroy her."

"Yes, Akdor. I will. And if I do, what will be my reward?"

"You will be made a sub-visser. How many troops will you need?"

"None, Akdor. I will go as a spy, not a conqueror. I will pass as a Hork-Bajir. I will find the Andalite. And I will kill her."

But of course, I was lying. You see, I had already realized one very important thing: From now on, the host body one had would be an indication of power. Already there were lines of distinction between Yeerks who had Gedd hosts and Yeerks who were given the new, powerful Hork-Bajir bodies.

These Hork-Bajir would be our shock troops.

But there was still one host better than Hork-Bajir: Andalite.

Yes, the Yeerk who could take an Andalite host would be more than a mere *sub*-visser. The Yeerk who could take and hold an Andalite host would be a visser, at the very least. And someday, who knows? A seat on the Council of Thirteen?

"I will take care of this matter, Akdor," I said. "I will deal with the Andalite."

chapter 19

ALDREA

Father Deep. That's what the Hork-Bajir called it. They thought it was the land of monsters, below the mist. But the zone of monsters was fairly narrow.

I now had some understanding of the layout. The upper valley, above the blue mist barrier, was Hork-Bajir land. A land of steep inclines and gigantic trees.

Beneath the mist was a somewhat more level belt that encircled the valley. In this zone of dense fog and eerie plants, the monsters lived.

Now we were in the third zone: no longer a steep valley, but sheer cliffs. Cliffs that were covered by a complex of walkways, stairways, arches, carved-out plazas, homes, businesses. . . . They had every imaginable feature of a moderately advanced civilization but one: They were empty. No one seemed to be living here.

<I would cut off my tail for a portable sensor,> I said.

"What is a portable sensor?"

<It's a device you can carry that performs a number of functions. It would tell us how old this place is. I don't know if all this was created last week, last millennium, or at the dawn of history.>

We were descending the cliff face by an endlessly long stairway. Every few dozen feet, the stairway would broaden out into a landing. A walkway would cross the landing. Along the walkways we could see doorways.

I was primed. Ready. Expecting attack at any moment. But the silence seemed to speak of emptiness. Emptiness everywhere in the valley around and below us.

Not that I wanted to think about what was below us. If I strayed off the steps, I'd fall. I'd fall for a very long time, down, down till I hit the exposed core of the planet.

Of course, long before I hit actual bottom I'd be incinerated. But that wasn't a very comforting thought.

We reached yet another landing and we both froze. This walkway was different. It was broader by far, chiseled deeper into the cliff. And a hundred feet down the walkway we could see some sort of vast opening.

<Shall we investigate it?>

"Why not?"

So we headed down along the walkway. And there, on our right, we came upon the opening. An opening so vast it could have been a hangar for a fleet of ships.

We stepped into the opening. It was nice to move away from the cliff face and that precipitous drop. But the size of this space was intimidating. I felt I should bow my head. You could play three separate games of driftball at once in that space. The sound of my hooves echoed off stone walls I could not even see in the gloom.

<What do you suppose this place is?> I asked.

Dak just shook his head. He was looking up in wonder, searching for the roof we knew was above us but couldn't see in the deep shadows.

<It's an open place, at least,> I said. <We could stay the night here. We need rest. And I don't think the Yeerks will come after us anymore tonight. Even if they did, how would they find us in this absurd maze of walkways and openings?>

"It would be good to rest," Dak said. "We cannot stay in any of the smaller dwellings we saw. Too small. Too confining."

I certainly agreed with that. No one wanted walls around them and roofs above them if they could avoid it. On board a spacecraft it was inevitable, but this space was so large it might almost have been an open field.

<No grass,> I grumbled.

"No trees," Dak said. "And the flat, horizontal angle of the floor is disturbing to me."

<But, on the positive side, no Yeerks.>

"Yes. We can sleep here."

<I will take the first watch,> I said.

Dak slept as Hork-Bajir do: He relaxed his legs and slumped down into a sort of sitting position, with legs splayed out in front and thick tail providing a third support. His head fell forward, chin to chest.

He was asleep instantly, as far as I could tell. I was jealous. Sleep isn't always that easy for me. For most Andalites. We are a watchful species. My mother explained it to me once when I found myself unable to sleep for several days.

<We no longer have predators to attack us,> she'd said, <but evolution does not just throw away adaptations that were necessary once. The animals we evolved from were prey for millions of years. They lived in vast herds, always watched by hungry predators. This was before we developed our tail blades and we had no protection but speed. We still feel the need to watch for predators. It may be a million years before we lose that instinct.>

My mother was good at explaining things like that. It's what she did. She was a scientist. Like I was supposed to be.

But now she was dead. In part because we An-

107

dalites had begun to forget that instinct for caution. We had forgotten that even though the predators on our own world had died out, there were still predators loose in the galaxy.

Or at least parasites.

I stood there in the gloom, in the faint reflected glow from the valley floor, and I remembered the searing light of the shredders as they ripped my family apart, atom by atom by atom.

I had to find a way to contact the fleet or the home world. Nothing would save this planet now but the appearance of a full-fledged Andalite war fleet.

That meant Z-space communication. A radio signal would take decades to reach anyone. I needed advanced Zero-space transponders.

And the only ones on this planet were aboard the ships the Yeerks controlled.

No need for concern, Aldrea, I said to myself. *Just walk up to the nearest Yeerk landing area, tell them you want to borrow the fighter, initiate contact with the home world, and suggest they rush directly to our assistance. Nothing whatever to worry about.*

I looked at Dak, asleep, his forehead horns raked forward, arms bent to keep the blades outward. *He would be hard to attack while sleeping,* I thought. From behind, the tail spikes. From the sides, the arm blades. From the front, the horns.

He'd said he would do anything for me. He'd said it in a way that . . . no, that was ridiculous. We were different species. Totally, completely different.

And yet I enjoyed spending time with him. I enjoyed talking with him. I missed him when we were separated.

Perfect, Aldrea, I laughed to myself. *He's covered with blades; he'll soon be seven feet tall; he eats with his mouth; and he swings through the trees.*

I was just lonely, that was it. There were no Andalite males around, and I was at the appropriate age for an interest in males. If there had been an interesting Andalite around, I'd have cared nothing about Dak.

There are no Andalite males, I reminded myself, *and even if there were, you have no choice but to care about Dak. At the very best, the fleet would take two months to arrive. And this strange, bladed creature is your only friend.*

Two months. If I could reach my people. If.

And if I could not reach my people, could Dak reach his? Could the simple, placid Hork-Bajir be made to rise up and save themselves?

Was Dak Hamee the seer ready to become Dak Hamee the general?

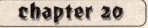

DAK HAMEE

In the middle of the night I woke. I told Aldrea to sleep. And I waited.

I did more thinking that night than I had ever done in my life. I had seen amazing things. I had seen terrible things. And now I understood that I had to do more than just follow Aldrea.

I did not believe Aldrea was bad, not in the way the Yeerks were bad. But Aldrea had lied to me. Aldrea was an Andalite first, my friend second. And she was hungry for revenge against the Yeerks.

It was up to me to figure out what to do to save my people. But I had no ideas. No Hork-Bajir had ever faced this problem before. I was helpless.

I stood, thinking, for hours. Then, slowly, the diffuse light from below was replaced by a brighter, cleaner light from above.

It took me a while before I realized that somehow, the light really was from above, even though I

110

knew there were thousands of feet of rock above me.

I craned my neck back and looked up.

"Aldrea! Wake up!"

Aldrea's eyes snapped open. All four of them. The stalk eyes slowly turned to look upward.

There, in the center of the vast, domed roof, was a hole. The hole was the bottom of a shaft. The shaft was as big as the trunk of the Tribe Tree.

Without speaking, we moved beneath the shaft and looked straight up. Up into clear, open sky, thousands of feet above us. So far away that the circle of sky looked smaller than Aldrea's eye.

But the shaft itself was filled with light. It glittered. It seemed almost to be alive, as though the walls of the shaft were moving and each movement sparkled.

<Like diamonds,> Aldrea said.

Light glowed from the shaft, and slowly the walls of the vast cavern became visible. I had expected smooth, gray or tan rock. But this was not mere rock. The walls of the cavern were covered entirely in swatches and patterns of strange colors. Blues, greens, oranges. Not smooth at all, but quilted.

Peering closer, I could see that all the patches of color were of a similar shape: short wings . . . arms . . . feet . . . heads!

<They're alive!> Aldrea cried.

The walls of the cavern were covered in living creatures of every imaginable shade.

Then, in a moment I shall remember for all of my life, the creatures woke up. At the same instant, ten thousand eyes opened. Each glittered like a star. Ten thousand glittering eyes stared down at us from left and right and above.

Down they came, slowing their fall with their short wings. Each of them was no more than half my height, but there were so many!

They fell and fell and fell, landing noiselessly. They stood on four legs. They had two elongated arms. They had faces dominated by the glittering eyes and small, red mouths.

"They're *chadoos*!" I blurted. "Like large *chadoos*. But so colorful!"

<Not *chadoos*, just distant relatives, I think,> Aldrea said.

The creatures began to walk past us, ignoring us as if we weren't there. They were heading calmly out of the cavern, turning left or right along the walkway outside.

But half a dozen of the creatures headed straight for us. One in brilliant purple spoke.

"What are you doing here?" he asked.

"He speaks my language," I said to Aldrea.

"How I communicate is irrelevant," he or she

112

said. "You heard me. You understand. Therefore, answer my question."

"We are . . . I mean, I am from above."

"Yes, yes, I'm not an idiot. You are a Hork-Bajir. What are you doing here, Hork-Bajir? There are no trees here. There is no bark for you to eat."

I shrugged. I looked at Aldrea, waiting for her to jump in. But she seemed as taken aback as I was. "They were chasing us. We came here to escape."

"*Who* was chasing you?"

<Yeerks,> Aldrea said.

"What are you?" the creature asked Aldrea.

<I am Andalite.>

"This is not your place, Andalite. It is not your place, Hork-Bajir. Leave."

The creature turned and began to walk away.

"No," I said.

The creature stopped.

"No?"

"No," I said firmly. "You will explain who you are. What this place is."

"We are the Arn," the creature said. "I am named Quatzhinnikon."

<Do you realize that the Hork-Bajir don't even know you exist?> Aldrea demanded.

"Of course they don't. We don't want them to know. That's why we created the various species of creatures who live in the zone of separation. We

wanted to keep the Hork-Bajir on their side of the zone. Now I must go. I have work to do."

He started once again to leave. I grabbed him. I wasn't rough, but I was firm.

"Ahh! Ahhh!" Quatzhinnikon cried. A dozen Arn turned to stare. They were horrified, afraid.

"Answer our questions," I said.

"Are you threatening me?" Quatzhinnikon whimpered.

I started to say "No, of course not." But Aldrea answered for me.

<Yes, we're threatening you, and you appear to be appropriately frightened. So answer our questions and spare us the arrogance.>

Quatzhinnikon gave her a poisonous look with his glittering, diamond eyes. "You are not part of the balance. You will upset everything. I will not help you."

In a flash, Aldrea's tail was at the small creature's throat. <We're in a hurry. We don't have time to be diplomatic. So let me make this simple for you: Answer us, or I will twitch my tail and your head will go rolling across this floor. Do you understand?>

I can't say I was completely shocked. I'd begun to get a fuller picture of Andalites in general and Aldrea in particular. But Quatzhinnikon was definitely shocked.

"Everything will fail now," he moaned. "The careful balance we've built!"

But he told us what we wanted to know. He answered our questions.

When he was done, I wished he hadn't.

chapter 21

ALDREA

We went to a different place, along a walkway, down more stairs. Just another Arn hole in the wall, at first. But then Quatzhinnikon touched a blue pad set into one wall.

The wall opened.

Behind the wall was a long, long room, dug deep into the bedrock. The room was filled with row after row of long cylinders. The cylinders were covered in dust. It had been a very long time since anyone had been there.

Quatzhinnikon walked past the cylinders, row after row of them. At the far end of the room I saw what could only be a large computer console.

<Well, well,> I said. <Not simple cave dwellers after all, are you?>

Quatzhinnikon went to the console and stepped confidently up to a bank of strange controls. He pressed several buttons. And on the wall behind him, a huge viewscreen appeared.

It showed a lush, green and blue planet in orbit around a red giant star.

"Twelve thousand years ago," Quatzhinnikon said.

The screen showed something new twirling through space. An asteroid. It was impossible to judge the relative size, but it was big.

"An asteroid in unstable orbit," Quatzhinnikon explained. "Each year, another near miss. We knew it would hit us. We tried to build spacecraft to escape. But we failed to manage anything more than local spaceflight. We were interested in biology, not physics. We made it as far as the uninhabitable second moon. No farther. So all we could do was wait. And recalculate the orbit and wait some more. And then . . ."

On the screen we saw the asteroid suddenly plow straight into the planet. The impact was shocking. The entire planet shuddered. Pieces of it went flying off into space. A vast cloud of dust and smoke enveloped the planet, slowly settling over the course of years.

When the dust and smoke cleared, the planet was very much changed. Huge cracks had formed from the impact of the asteroid. Huge cracks that formed a belt of valleys around the planet.

"Much of the atmosphere was gone," Quatzhinnikon explained. "A few thousand of us had

117

waited on the moon, frozen in stasis. We awoke to find that." He pointed at the planet.

"We returned to our home world to find everyone dead. Our entire species. The air was unbreathable, except in the valleys. But even there, the balance was precarious. A hair too much carbon dioxide, a shade too little nitrogen, and even the impact valleys would die.

"So we went to work to understand this new environment. We needed a mechanism for controlling the atmosphere."

<The trees,> I said. I knew then where this was going. I turned one stalk eye to look at Dak. He had not figured it out yet. Should I silence the Arn? Should I stop him before he revealed the truth to Dak?

"Yes, of course. The trees," Quatzhinnikon agreed. "Different species, each subtly different in its use of carbon dioxide and its production of oxygen. The perfect balance, the perfect mix, that's what we needed. But they would require constant care. And we were not willing to become a race of tree-herders."

Quatzhinnikon seemed to hesitate. As if he had read the doubts in my own mind. Should Dak know the truth?

<So you created a race of tree-herders,> I said. <Right here, in this room.>

"Yes. In this room we used all our genetic skill to design and build a species that would be perfectly adapted to caring for the trees, preserving them. We made them bark-eaters. We gave them bodies perfectly adapted to the task."

Dak's eyes widened. He looked at me, disbelief on his face. I nodded slightly.

<Yes, Dak,> I said. <This is your creator.>

Dak looked at the Arn in shock. But he did not fall to his knees or tremble in awe. He was surprised, not impressed.

<Why the monsters?> I asked.

"To keep the Hork-Bajir separate from us," Quatzhinnikon said. "You see, intelligence was not necessary for tree-herders. The Hork-Bajir, as we called them, were intellectually inferior. We felt it was best if they lived in ignorance of us. So for twelve thousand years they have lived beyond the blue mist, kept away by the genetically engineered horrors they call monsters."

I swear I was ready to show the self-satisfied creature my tail blade. <You arrogant, contempt-ible —> I began.

To my surprise, Dak cut me off with a raised hand. "You created the Hork-Bajir?"

"Yes," Quatzhinnikon said. "Or at least my people did."

"Then you need us," Dak said flatly.

119

Quatzhinnikon looked warily at the towering Hork-Bajir. "Yes. I suppose that's true."

"The Hork-Bajir will be destroyed. Enslaved and taken from this planet," Dak said. "You will lose your tree-herders. The Yeerks are already destroying us."

Quatzhinnikon shrugged. "What can we do? We have no weapons."

"The monsters," Dak said. "You control them, don't you? How else would you be able to keep them within the narrow band that separates your people from mine?"

Now it was my turn to be surprised. That had not occurred to me. But Dak was right! The Arn had control of the so-called monsters.

Quatzhinnikon gave Dak a hard look. "Of course. You're one of the smart ones, aren't you? A seer. We never could entirely eradicate that one bundle of genes. We did our best, but still, from time to time, one of you will arise."

"Yes, I am a seer," Dak said calmly.

"You're a freak, is what you are," Quatzhinnikon said. "A dangerously unstable element. It was our one great failure: One in ten thousand Hork-Bajir is born with intelligence that rivals that of the Arn."

"How do you control the monsters?" Dak asked.

"You'll ruin everything!"

"I will save my people," Dak said. "In saving them, I may save yours as well. The Yeerks will not be frightened off by the blue mist and children's stories of Father Deep. They will come for you next. Help us now and you may live."

Later I complimented Dak. <You have learned to go right to the point. You've learned to always keep your own goals in mind and not be distracted.>

"Yes," he said. "I am beginning to learn ruthlessness. I have had a very good example to follow."

I knew what he meant. But I wasn't going to acknowledge it. What could I do? Laugh and say, <Yes, we Andalites certainly are good teachers when it comes to ruthless self-interest.> It might have been true, but it would have been stupid to admit it.

He'd caught me off guard. I didn't know what to say. <Y-y-yes, the, um, the Yeerks are good examples of ruthlessness, aren't they?> I stammered.

Dak smiled.

chapter 22

ESPLIN 9466

Fitting in with the Hork-Bajir had been pitifully easy. The host body I'd taken was named Fet Mashar. His friends had seen him taken into a fighter. They had seen him being dragged away by Gedds.

And yet when I reappeared among them very few questions were asked. I simply said, "I am back." And the Hork-Bajir would say, "Yes, you are back."

I began to realize that we Yeerks would have a very great advantage as we went conquering through the galaxy. We might come across races that were smarter, more powerful, more dangerous than the Hork-Bajir. In those cases, we could infiltrate slowly. Take one host at a time, build slowly, never letting our victims know what was happening until it was too late.

But those tactics were hardly necessary here. We

were able to simply set up a ground base and do business in the open. We were capturing and infesting a hundred Hork-Bajir a day. That number would rise every day as we acquired more and more Hork-Bajir hosts to do the hard work.

In fact, even my efforts to infiltrate the Hork-Bajir were unnecessary. The first Hork-Bajir I asked gave me the name of Dak Hamee as the Hork-Bajir who'd been in touch with the Andalites.

Dak Hamee and a friend of his named Jagil. We looked for Jagil to infest him, but he couldn't be found. Nevertheless, we were soon quite sure of the name Dak Hamee.

Dak Hamee was not my main concern, though. It was the Andalite I wanted. And I learned her name, too.

Aldrea. She was, as she had said, the daughter of Prince Seerow.

The irony was too perfect. The fool Seerow, who had blathered on about peace and brotherhood while Akdor and the others had prepared to attack, had a daughter. Obviously, the daughter was less a fool than her father had been.

But had she somehow survived the trip into the mist? No one had seen her these last two days. There would be an armed expedition into the mist once we were strong enough. For now there was the simple work of rounding up Hork-Bajir from all over the valley and bringing them to our hastily dug Yeerk pool.

This new Yeerk pool had not been easy to create. The ground was at such a slant we'd have had to dig out thousands of tons of dirt. So a better way was found. We used a shredder to cut down a big, hollow tree the Hork-Bajir used to communicate. The tree fell sideways, landing level. It rolled to a stop, held back by the other trees. After that it was a simple matter to burn away the outer covering on the top, creating a very long, narrow Yeerk pool.

It was, actually, an impressive sight. The tree was over a thousand feet long to begin with. We burned away most of that, but it still left us with a two-hundred-foot-long log. Lying on its side, the trunk towered overhead, more than sixty feet. We built stairs going up one side and down the other, with narrow platforms around the open pool.

We did all that. But we did not mount shredder cannon on this log. Nor did we keep a secure perimeter. Why bother? The Hork-Bajir were completely harmless.

I was not in command of the Yeerk pool. I was not responsible for what came next. Although, to be honest, I wouldn't have thought to do anything different. Still, I wasn't blamed. The Yeerk who was blamed was later executed. He was slowly starved of Kandrona rays. Very slowly. It took him weeks to die.

However, I was *there* that terrible evening. I was there, laughing and joking with other excited new Hork-Bajir-Controllers. We all loved these host bodies. We were all sure these hosts would make us the match of Andalites in personal combat.

With these bodies we could build the things we could never have built with clumsy Gedd hosts. We would build our own weapons. Our own ships! Vast, powerful ships that would make the galaxy tremble.

All the races of the galaxy would be our hosts. Our slaves. And when we were strong enough, we would go after the arrogant overlords, the meddling fools whose fleet kept our home world imprisoned. In our lifetimes we would attack, defeat, and enslave the Andalites.

It all seemed so easy then. Ten minutes later, we knew better.

I was standing by the edge of the pool, joking with my twin. Yes, of course, I am a twin. But I am the primary. He is the secondary.

We were talking about tactics for fighting with Hork-Bajir blades when we heard the cries.

I peered into the darkness beneath the towering trees.

"Aaarrrgghh! Aaahhh! Help! Help!"

The cries of several voices. All terrified. All panicked. Followed by the sizzling noise of shredder fire. And beneath all that, a low rumbling roar.

I saw Hork-Bajir and Gedds running our way. Stumbling as they ran. I loosened my shredder in its holster.

And then they appeared. You can have no possible idea how horrifying that sight was.

A line of creatures advanced. But creatures like nothing I had ever imagined. Huge, freakish, foul creatures with twisted bodies and massive hands and bristling horns.

But as frightening as this weird army was, what frightened me more, what made it all seem terribly dangerous, was a small, bluish-purple figure standing at the head of this mob.

A single Andalite girl. Beside her stood a lumbering Hork-Bajir I assumed must be Dak Hamee.

It was Aldrea. The daughter of Seerow.

She seemed beautiful to me. Is that strange? I suppose it is. But there is a compelling beauty in the sight of someone seemingly so small and yet so dangerous.

And even I, her enemy, could not help being impressed by the sweet irony of it all. Seerow, who had freed us without knowing his peril, was now replaced by Aldrea, who would send us back to the Yeerk pools. Or to death.

126

Yes, there was something beautiful in that small, delicate, dangerous creature.

Someday, I would tell her how I'd felt at this awful moment. Someday, I would live inside her head and I would tell her that I had admired her on this day.

Someday, when she was my host.

chapter 23

ALDREA

It took us a day to learn the mind-control techniques the Arn used to control their monsters. Mind-amplifier implants were placed just under the skin of our scalps. We trained at broadcasting simple commands and simple images to the genetic freaks the Arn had created.

It took another two days to assemble the creatures from all around the valley. In the end, we had more than a hundred.

They were a circus of twisted DNA. The Arn had not missed a trick.

The *Jubba-Jubba*, like the three-fingered monstrosity that had attacked us.

The *Galilash*, fourteen feet tall, with green-and-red reptilian flesh and razored tentacles.

The *Gorks*, only three feet tall but twenty feet across, shuffling, twelve-legged horrors with snapping, extending mouths on all sides.

There was a monster called a *Lerdethak*, a bizarre tangle of living vines surrounding a ravening mouth.

And then there were things the Hork-Bajir had never seen long enough to name. Things with mouths that could chew down a tree, things with needle-sharp quills ten feet long, things that squirted acid.

It was a sad, sick collection. In a better world, a world of peace and justice, someone would have punished the Arn for what they had done. Twisting life to make monsters is an evil thing to do.

But their evil served our purpose.

We had an army.

We advanced up the slope, up out of the mist. A hundred nightmares behind Dak and me. Silent and relentless, we advanced.

<I hope I get the opportunity to see the expression on the faces of the Yeerks who see us first,> I said. <I want to see what they think of this!>

"They will be afraid," Dak said. "So will my people."

<You have to try and get your people to come along with us. To fight beside us.>

"How do I do this?"

<Show them. Show them what to do and they will do it.>

We had miles to climb before we'd reach the Yeerk camp. Hork-Bajir hid in the trees above us, cowering, staring, whimpering as the army of terror marched beneath them.

<Call up to them, Dak,> I said. <You are their seer. This is your moment!>

He gave me a look I'd seen more and more often from him. A look of sullen anger, resentment.

That was to be expected. I understood. He resisted turning to violence. That just meant he was a decent creature. But he would come to see the necessity of fighting. He would see I was correct. When the Yeerks were destroyed and his people were free once more, he would see.

<Call up to them. Tell them not to be afraid,> I said again.

Dak raised his face up to the trees. "Do not fear! I am Dak Hamee. I am the seer, sent to teach and to lead. Do not be afraid! These monsters will not harm you. We go to destroy the invaders! We go to kill the Yeerks!"

Still the Hork-Bajir clung to the bark and the branches.

"Follow us," Dak cried. "Stay in the trees, but follow us! Watch us and learn!"

<Watch your seer!> I yelled in bold thought-speak. <Watch him and do as he does. He is the seer! The seer has been sent to lead you. Watch him and do as *he* does. Watch Dak Hamee, and do as *he* does! Do as *he* does! Do as *he* does!>

"You've come to understand we Hork-Bajir very well in so short a time," Dak said coldly. "A simple, repeated message for a simple people."

<They need to understand,> I said. <We are getting close.>

I could feel the Yeerk camp ahead of us. I could smell the stale stink of the Yeerk pool.

<When the battle begins I will race for the closest parked spacecraft,> I explained. <The most important thing is that we get a message out to the Andalite fleet. Everything rests on that. It will be up to you to carry on the battle, once it has started. You must not weaken. Attack, attack, attack. Don't give the Yeerks a chance to regroup. Don't forget: The Hork-Bajir in that camp are not Hork-Bajir. They are Yeerks.>

Dak nodded his horned head. "Have you fought in many battles, Aldrea?"

I was surprised by the question. <No. Of course not. But I have studied —>

"Have you ever killed a fellow Andalite?"

<No! Why would you —>

"You ask me to kill my own people today and to lead my people in killing their brothers," Dak said. "You say they are not Hork-Bajir, but Yeerks. But when the dead have given up their souls to Mother Sky, there will be Hork-Bajir bodies lying dead."

<Dak, we've been over this and over this!> I ex-

ploded. <It's too late to be worrying about all that. This is a war! If you want your people to survive, you will —>

"Be quiet, Aldrea," Dak said.

He didn't shout. He said it calmly, in a low voice.

"These are *my* people who will die today. Be quiet, Andalite. Be quiet."

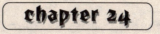

DAK HAMEE

We marched up the valley. We marched beneath the trees. In the branches overhead, more and more Hork-Bajir were following us. Hundreds now. All watching, waiting.

They were chanting as they swung from branch to branch. They were chanting "Do as *he* does. Do as *he* does."

Aldrea had done her job well. She had created a simple instruction for my fellow Hork-Bajir. She was very clever. The Andalites are a very clever species. Like the Yeerks. Like the Arn.

We had been created by one brilliant species, invaded and enslaved by another. And now a third was using us.

But as I marched I saw no way out. That was what made me feel as sick as someone who has eaten yellow bark. There was no other way for us. We had become tools to be used by smarter, more powerful species.

"Do as *he* does, do as *he* does."

Suddenly, they were right there in front of us. They had cut down the Speaking Tree. It lay across our path uphill, held in place by a pair of *Stoola* trees.

Hork-Bajir armed with shredders stood atop the felled *Nawin* tree and gaped down at us. Other Hork-Bajir fled before us, rushing back to their brothers. A few fired shredders at us. One monster lost an arm. It meant nothing.

We stopped just a few dozen yards from the felled tree. We could see the enemy clearly. They could see us.

There were only twenty or thirty Hork-Bajir-Controllers that I could see. But Aldrea had warned that more would arrive quickly. And, I knew, the Yeerk pool they'd built in the bowels of the felled tree would hold hundreds, perhaps thousands, of Yeerks in their natural state.

Beyond the tree, to the left, was a spacecraft. Aldrea said it had been an Andalite spacecraft. That was her goal.

She remained silent beside me, but I could feel her agitation, her eagerness.

"Are you ready, Aldrea?" I asked.

<Yes.>

I focused my mind as the Arn had taught us to do. I sent the simple instruction to the hulking army of monsters behind us. Their brains, simpler than even the simplest Hork-Bajir, understood the one-word order: Kill.

"Kill," I said, looking at Aldrea.

She did not look back at me. Instead she focused all her eyes forward. <For my mother. For my brother. For my father, Prince Seerow. KILL!>

We surged forward, a mass of demons. We surged up the hill. Great, powerful monsters, careless of gravity, bounded and slithered and shuffled and leaped at the Yeerks.

TSEEEW! TSEEEW!

Shredders fired.

RrrrAAAWWWRRRRR! A monster screamed as it burst into flame.

TSEEEW! TSEEEW!

I felt shredder blasts hit the ground beside me. But now I was running — terrified, but running forward.

TSEEEW! TSEEEW!

"Aaahhhh!" I cried as a near miss burned a semicircle in my shoulder.

<Attack!> Aldrea screamed.

TSEEEW! TSEEEW! TSEEEW! TSEEEW!

Shredder fire everywhere. A *Jubba-Jubba* exploded! A *Lerdethak* twisted, burning, writhing. But the monsters were under our control. They were incapable of running away.

Only a dozen yards to the felled tree.

Nine yards.

Five!

TSEEEW! TSEEEW!

Aldrea raced straight for the felled *Nawin* tree. The monsters were all around us. I felt I must be losing my mind.

"Aarrrrrggghhh!" A vast, yellow beast looked down to see a hole through its own stomach. A hole that smoked and sizzled.

We had reached the tree! It was a curved wall above us.

Up the stairs I ran, now screaming. Screaming in some mix of terror and hatred.

A *Jubba-Jubba* simply climbed up the side of the tree, passing me and leaping on the stunned defenders. The *Jubba-Jubba* grabbed the nearest Hork-Bajir-Controller, opened his vast mouth, and swallowed him from head to waist.

More monsters clambered up. Hork-Bajir-Controllers broke and ran. But others were rushing up from behind, trying to hold the line.

I was atop the *Nawin* tree. I could see the way the Yeerks had cut into it, opening it up to create a pool. It was not water — not water as I knew it, anyway. It was as dark as dirt, heavy, slow. And within it I saw flashes of slugs rippling here and there.

Yeerks. As Aldrea had told me. Those were Yeerks.

I stood atop the tree and looked around me. Aldrea racing for the parked fighter. Monsters killing and being killed. Hork-Bajir-Controllers firing shredders in panic as they were torn apart. Screaming, roaring, crying, shouting!

And up in the trees, hundreds of my fellow Hork-Bajir, all watching. Not understanding, but watching to see what I would do.

"Do as *he* does," they murmured still.

"Die!"

A shout from behind me. I spun. A Hork-Bajir-Controller, rushing at me, blades flashing.

I ducked beneath the swinging arc of his wrist blade.

I rose up, pushed his head back, and kicked into his stomach with my foot. The claws opened him up. He fell from the tree, rolled down the side, and landed at the feet of a *Galilash*. The *Galilash* . . .

It doesn't matter what the *Galilash* did.

What matters is that my people, the people I was to lead as seer, had seen what I did.

"Do as *he* does!" they cried.

They began to drop from the trees. And then the final horror began.

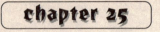

chapter 25

ALDREA

The battle raged!

I raced along the front of the log Yeerk pool. Between raging monsters and shouting, shredder-firing Hork-Bajir-Controllers.

I had never experienced anything like it before. It was not what I had expected. The shouts and cries. The moans of pain. Brilliant explosions going off everywhere. The smell of charred flesh.

I ran in panic, only barely remembering my goal. I reached the end of the log and turned right, racing uphill again toward the fighter that was parked there.

No guards! The Yeerks who should have been protecting the fighter had rushed to join the battle. A fatal mistake!

I ran for the fighter. The Yeerks had even left the hatch open. It was incredible. So easy!

I plowed inside, skidding to a halt. The noise of

battle seemed farther off now. Like it was happening somewhere else entirely. I heard less shredder fire.

Focus, Aldrea, I told myself. I was trembling. I stood before the communications panel. The Yeerks had altered some of the controls, but it was still basically a familiar Andalite panel.

<Computer, activate communications array,> I ordered. <Outgoing message. First address: Andalite home world. Priority one, two-way communication demanded. Second address: Andalite space fleet. Priority one, two-way communication demanded.>

<Ready,> the computer said.

<Open channels,> I said.

<Channels open. Begin message.>

I faced the panel. I tried to compose my expression. I knew I must look pretty wild. More to the point, I looked young. And female. The Andalite military was almost entirely male.

<This is Aldrea-Iskillion-Falan. I am communicating from the Hork-Bajir home world. I —>

Out of the corner of one stalk eye I saw the threatening shape loom up behind me. I spun and whipped my tail around. But the Hork-Bajir-Controller was quick. He blocked my tail blade.

He delivered a backhanded blow that connected solidly with my face. My legs buckled. I fell to my knees.

"I don't think I can allow you to call for help, Aldrea, daughter of Seerow."

My head was spinning. But even as I slumped over onto the deck, I thought, *Why isn't he using his blades on me? He could easily destroy me.*

The Hork-Bajir-Controller pressed one of his claw feet down on my upper body, pinning me down, helpless, unable to reach him with my tail.

"Computer. Terminate communication."

<Communication terminated.>

The Hork-Bajir-Controller looked down at me. "You've caused a lot of trouble, Andalite. Your friends are busily butchering my people out there."

<Go ahead. You want to kill me. Go ahead!> I cried with a lot more courage than I really felt. I was sick with fear. And just plain sick from the spinning in my head.

"Kill you? No, no, no. Not me," he said. "I don't want to kill you. I want to make you my host. I will be the first Andalite-Controller ever. I will have complete access to your every secret, to all the scientific and technical knowledge you possess. See, I've studied you Andalites. I admire you."

He didn't want to kill me? Then there might be time. Just maybe enough time. I had to stall him. Distract —

WHUMPF! The kick came without warning.

<Argghhh!> I groaned. I nearly passed out.

140

"Terribly sorry, but I need you to stay put. I'm going to power up this fighter and use its shredders to cut down your little army of DNA mistakes."

The kick had knocked the wind out of me. I think I actually did pass out, but only briefly. I couldn't move, but I could still think. And what I thought of was a single, simple picture.

The picture of a *Jubba-Jubba* monster.

The Yeerk was busy powering up the shredders. And then busy using the fighter's maneuvering thrusters to turn it toward the battle, bringing the shredders to bear.

One blast from the powerful shredders at this point-blank range would end the battle. He was actually laughing to himself as he brought the weapons around.

Then he noticed.

"Aaahhh!" He jumped back, eyes wide in disbelief.

I was halfway morphed. Halfway morphed into a *Jubba-Jubba* monster.

<I don't guess you Yeerks know about this bit of new technology yet,> I said.

"What are you doing?"

I reached for him and closed my huge, three-fingered hand around his neck.

<What am I doing? Destroying you, Yeerk. This is for my brother. For my mother. And for my *fa-*

ther.> I tightened my grip. The power in my hand was incredible! I could easily have ripped him apart. I felt the dull monster mind, barely more than a flicker of simplest intelligence, not even sentient. I felt its blunt violence. Its powerful DNA-encoded urge to destroy.

But I had practiced the morph. I knew how to dominate the monster's instincts. I knew how to keep my own Andalite mind in complete control. And that proved to be a mistake.

The monster would have snuffed out the life of the Yeerk without a second thought. But I was an Andalite. We are not beasts. The Hork-Bajir-Controller's tongue lolled out. He flailed helplessly. His eyes rolled up into his head. He stopped thrashing.

I released my pressure. And I still felt the life in his neck.

I carried him to the hatch and threw him outside. I closed the hatch and secured it. And then I demorphed.

<Computer, resume previous communication.>
<Begin message.>

<This is Aldrea-Iskillion-Falan. I am communicating from the Hork-Bajir world. Designation Sector Five, RG-Two-One-Five-Seven-Eight-Four. Prince Seerow, his wife, and son have been killed. I am his daughter.>

A face had appeared on the screen before me. A young warrior, oozing arrogance.

<The announcement of Prince Seerow's death is hardly a priority-one message,> he sneered. <Priority one is reserved for messages of the utmost —>

I was not feeling patient. I'd been punched, kicked, and stomped. <Then maybe this will be important enough for you: The Yeerks are here. Here in force, in orbit, and on the ground.>

The young warrior nearly fell over. <What?>

<I said the Yeerks are *here*.>

chapter 26

DAK HAMEE

The monsters were cut down, one by one, falling over each other, piles of twisted, hideous flesh.

But the Hork-Bajir dropped from the trees and did as I had shown them: They attacked the Hork-Bajir-Controllers. The first battle in all the history of our people. The first time any Hork-Bajir had killed another.

I saw the parked fighter begin to turn. Then it stopped.

I saw a fighter come swooping down from the sky. It hovered above the trees, but did not open fire. The reason was simple: It did not know whom to shoot. Or how. Both sides were intermingled in terrifying hand-to-hand combat.

Then the parked fighter began to turn again. The swooping shredder mounts came to bear on us. I waited, wondering who was holding the trigger of those powerful weapons.

Then, a faint thought-speak voice, weak from being so far away. <Dak! Get off the log! Get all your people off the log!>

"Everyone down! Follow me!" I yelled. I leaped to the ground and dozens of my people followed. We ran a short distance down the hill. The Yeerks atop the log cheered. They thought we were retreating.

The fighter fired.

TSEEEEEEW! TSEEEEEW!

The shredder beams sliced into and through the *Nawin* tree. The beams hit the liquid of the Yeerk pool inside. A huge explosion of steam followed.

"Aaaaarrrrrgggggghhhhh!" Hork-Bajir-Controllers screamed. They fell. Some ran away. Others struggled to get to their feet but were jumped by four, five, six of my fellow Hork-Bajir.

Suddenly, the log broke in two. It broke open, gushing the contents of the Yeerk pool out onto the ground. The heavy gray water rolled down toward us like the runoff from a rainstorm.

It washed over my feet. Over my toes. But it left behind a pile of slithering, squirming slugs. The Yeerks of the pool were now helpless upon the ground.

I did not give the order. My friend Jagil did. Gentle, fearful Jagil. He had learned a great deal in twenty minutes of combat.

"Kill them!" he cried. "Kill them! Do as Dak Hamee has done. Kill them!"

The remaining Controllers ran. Ran for their lives. Ran screaming through the trees. I don't know how many survived. Maybe none.

And my people set about stomping and cutting up the Yeerks who lay on the ground. It was like some nightmare dance.

Now, at last, the hovering fighter had found a target. It fired at the parked fighter. The blast annihilated the parked ship's shredders. The hatch opened and Aldrea came running out just as the hovering ship fired again and blew the grounded ship apart.

More fighters were coming down. They were landing and disgorging fresh Hork-Bajir-Controllers and Gedd-Controllers.

Aldrea came running, breathless. <Time to get out of here!> she cried. <We've accomplished what we wanted.>

I watched her as she realized what was happening to the Yeerk slugs. What my people were doing to them. Her face changed color. Her breathing stopped. She would not look at me.

"Yes, quite an accomplishment," I said.

<We have to get out of here,> she said in a flat tone.

"To the trees!" I roared to my people. "To the trees!"

They pulled back reluctantly from the slaughter. But they obeyed.

Obeyed. Me. Hork-Bajir who had never known the word "obedience" now obeyed me. Because I was the seer? Because I was wiser than they? No. Because I had destroyed their past and now they had no choice but to follow me into a future they could not imagine.

The monsters in our valley were destroyed that day. Only a very few survived. But that was all right, because we didn't need monsters anymore. We had become them.

chapter 27

ALDREA

Seven months passed, and the fleet did not come. Not the two months I had expected.

Perhaps Zero-space had shifted, leaving the Hork-Bajir home world farther away than it had been. That happens frequently. Or maybe the princes simply didn't believe me. Or maybe, maybe, maybe. I went through every "maybe" I could think of. And still the fleet did not come.

Seven months passed, during which Dak Hamee and I learned the techniques of guerrilla warfare: 1) Strike with the element of surprise at the enemy's weak point. 2) Withdraw before the counterattack can begin. 3) Use the population for support, regardless of reprisals.

We trained a hard core of Hork-Bajir. We called it the Hork-Bajir army. We captured Yeerk shredders. We attacked Yeerk ground bases. We hid in the trees or among the resentful, fearful Arn. We were brave and resourceful. But we were losing.

The Yeerks moved into other valleys. We spread the resistance, but we were never fast enough. The Yeerks were spreading through the Hork-Bajir like a virus. They had thousands, tens of thousands of Hork-Bajir hosts.

And we began to notice other things. The shredders we captured were being altered. The Yeerks called this new weapon a "Dracon beam." It did not kill as cleanly as a shredder. It caused more pain.

And even more ominous, huge excavations were occurring. The Yeerks were mining. Iron, uranium, nickel, bauxite. Diamonds and rubies. They were building stronger bases. And from the far side of the planet, we heard stories of vast constructions.

I had very little doubt *what* the Yeerks were building, and eventually we had proof: They were building more spacecraft. Craft that would be manned by Hork-Bajir-Controllers and armed with the new Dracon beam weapon.

The Yeerks had learned very fast. They had Andalite, Skrit Na, Ongachic, and Hawjabran technology to dissect. And now they were no longer held back by a lack of hosts.

It was a dark day. Mother Sky was weeping, sending down tears to soothe Father Deep's anger. It was raining.

Our little army came back from a harassing attack. We retreated to the dwellings of the Arn, carrying a badly wounded warrior.

Quatzhinnikon greeted us in the vast cavern where we had first met him. It was still daylight and his people were awake and about.

"Why have you come back here again?"

<We have a wounded warrior here,> I said. The Arn had lost none of their skill in biology. We'd suffered very few wounds they couldn't treat successfully.

"I have told you. You are not welcome here. You will bring your war to us."

"It will come anyway, Quatzhinnikon," Dak said. "The Yeerks are more powerful every day. How long do you think it will be until they tire of enslaving Hork-Bajir and begin making hosts of the Arn?"

The small, purple creature smiled smugly. "A very long time now, seer of the Hork-Bajir. We have been busy. We have not rested." He turned a cold, dismissive look on me. "And we have not put our faith in your never-appearing Andalite fleet, either. We no longer fear the Yeerks."

My first thought was that the Arn had invented some powerful weapon. But no, the Arn were not builders of weapons. They were creators of life, however twisted.

<Explain. But first, tend to this injured Hork-Bajir.>

"We have altered our own DNA," Quatzhinnikon said complacently. "We have altered our own physiology. We have weakened a blood vessel in our own brains to the point where any increase in cranial pressure will cause the vessel to rupture. Should a Yeerk attempt to enter any Arn brain, the vessel will rupture and the Arn will die. A dead host is of no use to the Yeerks. Therefore they will leave us in peace. All Arn in all the valleys of this world will be altered this way within days."

For a moment, I stared. Then I laughed. <Fool. Do you think the Yeerks will let you live here on a world they intend to possess?>

Quatzhinnikon shrugged. "They will have no use for us."

"Exactly," Dak said. "And what they do not need, they destroy."

Quatzhinnikon's complacent face twitched. "Leave this place. You will find no help here."

"I will kill him," Jagil said, glaring at Quatzhinnikon.

"No," Dak said. "The Yeerks will kill him."

"I will kill Yeerks," Jagil said. "I am a great Yeerk-killer!"

"Yes, you are, my friend," Dak said sadly.

151

"He is a great Yeerk-killer!" Delf Hajool echoed staunchly.

Dak smiled at Delf Hajool, who stood beside Jagil. Delf and Jagil had become a couple. The Hork-Bajir pair off earlier in life than we Andalites.

It was almost too painful to think of the future Jagil and Delf faced.

I looked at Dak and felt a wave of self-pity. No future for Jagil and Delf. No future for Dak and me. In some ways we had become even closer, fighting side by side. But the easy fun, the trust, of our earlier times was gone. I often recalled the time when I had morphed a *chadoo* and climbed to the top of the Tribe Tree. I held on to that memory.

We climbed wearily back up out of the Arn wall-city. We rested in the zone once inhabited by monsters and now empty. The wounded Hork-Bajir died. That night we found a tree away from any Yeerk concentrations. We dug a hole at the roots and buried him, in the Hork-Bajir tradition.

I looked around at our small army: forty-two Hork-Bajir and me. Thirty-one of us armed with older-model shredders or newer Dracon beams. None of us without scars.

We were winning small battles. We were losing the war. Soon there would not be enough of us left to carry on.

The rain had stopped and the night sky had

cleared by the time we emerged from the Arn wall-city.

"Mother Sky's flowers are strange tonight," a Hork-Bajir named Had Kalpak said.

I followed the direction of his gaze, turning one stalk eye skyward. Then, in a flash, all my eyes were lifted up.

Mother Sky's flowers were strange, all right. Up against the black of space I saw the swift-moving lights. And then, the bright beams of light and the tiny, silent, far-off explosion.

<Space battle!> I cried. <There's a space battle going on in orbit!>

Dak grabbed me, almost too roughly. "The Andalites?"

I laughed. I laughed and laughed and danced around. <Well, it sure isn't the Skrit Na up there frying Yeerks!> I cried. <They've come! They've come! Everything is going to be all right. The fleet is here!>

chapter 28

DAK HAMEE

Andalite fighters landed in the clearing where Aldrea's family had lived. They were battle-scarred. But when the hatches opened, the Andalites who stepped out seemed confident.

<You must be Aldrea-Iskillion-Falan,> one of them said. <Come with me. I'm Sofor. I'll take you to the prince.>

<I'm glad to see you,> Aldrea said. <This is Dak Hamee, the seer of the Hork-Bajir people.>

<Scary-looking brute,> Sofor said, looking me up and down. <Let's go, youngster. The prince is not known for his patience, and we had a hot welcome to this hellhole.>

"Fortunately, we *are* patient," I said, stepping forward. "We've waited seven months for you to get here."

<It speaks,> the Andalite warrior said. <Mouthsounds, of course.> He turned to Aldrea again. <Say

good-bye to your pet, young one, I have my orders.>

<Dak is coming with me,> Aldrea said.

"No," I interrupted. "I am not going with you. These are my people. This is my planet. And for seven months, it has been a Hork-Bajir war. You," I said, pointing at the arrogant Andalite, "you will tell your prince that we welcome him. We will be glad to meet him . . . when *he* comes *here*."

I turned and walked away. I didn't know if Aldrea would follow me. But after a few seconds I heard her hooves on the grass beside me.

<Was that wise, Dak? They've come to help.>

"No. They've come to kill Yeerks. Not to help."

<It's the same thing!>

I stopped walking. "Listen to me, Aldrea. We are going to end up being pawns in this war between Yeerks and Andalites."

<That's not going to happen. My people aren't like that,> she said.

"We'll see," I said.

Two hours later, a runner came swinging through the trees to tell me that a larger Andalite ship was landing in the clearing.

<Happy now?> Aldrea asked me.

I smiled. "It's a start."

We returned to the clearing. We were taken

aboard a rather beautiful Andalite warship unlike the others I'd seen. A name was on the hull in flowing Andalite script. It read *Jahar*.

On board a large, powerful Andalite stood waiting. He glared at us with a look that could have been a shredder beam.

<Alloran!> Aldrea gasped.

<What do you mean by summoning me down here? When I give an order I expect it to be obeyed!> he roared. <And it's War-Prince Alloran to you, female child!>

<My name is Aldrea-Iskillion-Falan. Daughter of Prince Seerow. This is Dak Hamee, seer of the Hork-Bajir people.>

<I know who you are,> Alloran said. <And I regret your family's death. You are no doubt to be commended for having hidden out for seven months. We will reward whoever took care of you. Was it you, Hork-Bajir? Anything you want. You have our official thanks for hiding this female.> To Sofor and his other officers he added, <Get us out of here. Standard orbit. Sensor sweep as soon as we clear the atmosphere. There may still be one or two Yeerk ships left flying.>

Aldrea turned a stalk eye toward me. I met her gaze and smiled.

She had once promised to take me flying. Of

course, it was a promise she'd intended as a bribe. And yet here it was, coming true at last.

But I had no time to enjoy the moment. That made me sad. There'd been little enough to enjoy over these last seven months. Now, however, I had more important matters to deal with. I had to remain totally unimpressed. I had to be the seer of my people.

"War-Prince Alloran," I said, in a friendly but not deferential tone. "You have a lot to learn. If you'd like, we can give you a briefing on the situation here."

<A briefing? Ahh-hah-hah-hah! You'll tell *me*!>

He and the other Andalites all laughed. I had to struggle to control my temper. Lately, I'd been having more and more trouble with anger.

"There are seventeen Yeerk ground bases spread through fourteen valleys," I said. "There are three known mining camps where the Yeerks are busy extracting iron, bauxite, nickel, tin, copper, and uranium, as well as various gemstones I'm told are useful for focusing shredders. The largest construction area is two valleys west of here. It is well-camouflaged, having been dug back into the slope of the valley. We suspect that they have built fourteen fighter craft, based on a new design but similar in capabilities to your own Andalite fighters. These fighters are armed with two Dracon beam weapons, a blending of Andalite shredder technology with some Ongachic particle-wave technology."

War-Prince Alloran stared. All the Andalites stared.

"Shall I continue?"

Alloran nodded his head slowly.

"The Yeerks are also constructing a new type of ship, quite large, very heavily armed. It seems almost to have been inspired by Hork-Bajir physiology. We . . . Aldrea and I . . . have taken to calling it a Blade ship."

<You've actually seen all this?> Sofor demanded.

<Yes,> Aldrea answered.

<How?>

"We have attacked several of these bases," I said. "Others we have infiltrated."

<Attacked Yeerk bases? What, the two of you?> Alloran said.

<No, War-Prince Alloran,> Aldrea said proudly. <We attacked with the Hork-Bajir army. That's what we've been doing for the last seven months. Not hiding out.>

"It has been a small army," I said. "We have had a total of eight hundred and twelve Hork-Bajir with us, at one time or another."

<And now?>

"Forty-two are with us now in this valley. Perhaps two hundred more are scattered in small groups in the other valleys. We have lost . . . many. Very many. I doubt we would have survived another month."

<You've taken seventy-percent casualties?> one of the other Andalites asked, awestruck.

"Yes." I closed my eyes. Had it been that many? Yes. Seven out of ten of the Hork-Bajir who'd rallied to me had died.

I gazed through a transparent panel and saw my own planet for the first time. Was that my own valley? Or had we passed over some other valley already? Did it matter? Weren't all Hork-Bajir one people?

<But now you're here,> Aldrea said enthusiastically. <Now we'll wipe the Yeerks off this planet!>

Alloran sighed. <We would, if we were still facing the handful of ships the Yeerks had before. But if what you tell us is true. . . . How many Hork-Bajir have been made into Yeerk hosts?>

<We don't know. We estimate they have perhaps forty thousand. Forty thousand Hork-Bajir hosts, maybe twelve of their new Bug fighters up and flying . . . that's what we call them. And the Blade ship, which we think is just coming online. Plus the Andalite and Skrit Na ships they already had.>

There was a long silence. A very long silence.

<But . . . but you'll destroy them,> Aldrea said hopefully.

<We have eight fighters, two transports, one re-supply ship, one repair ship. A total of less than a thousand warriors. We destroyed two Yeerk fighters on our way in.>

<But that's not enough!> Aldrea cried.

<Days after we heard your message from here we received intelligence reports that the Yeerk fleet was in Sector Two. The main fleet is there. We assumed that since . . . that because you . . .> He didn't finish.

<I'm just a female. And the daughter of Prince Seerow. So you assumed I was a fool,> Aldrea said flatly.

<It will take a year for the main fleet to get here, unless Z-space reconfigures,> one of the officers said.

<This is going to be a tough little war,> Alloran said grimly. <A very tough little war.>

<And it's starting right now!> Sofor cried. <We have multiple contacts, closing fast!>

chapter 29

ESPLIN 9466

"We have multiple contacts, Sub-Visser Twelve."

I heard the title and swelled with pleasure. I had been newly promoted. Up from Sub-Visser Seventeen, my first command rank. It was a jump of five places! Sub-Vissers Sixteen and Fourteen had been promoted. Sub-Visser Thirteen had been killed in battle against Hork-Bajir rebels. Sub-Visser Fifteen was being executed for incompetence and cowardice.

"Relay the sensor data to the Blade ship, Alahar-Seven-Eight-Six-Five," I ordered. It was just the two of us aboard the tiny Bug fighter. But I was in command. I was the twelfth highest-ranking sub-visser. Beyond that there were nine vissers. But every day there were promotions. Every day new sub-vissers and vissers were added. We were growing! These were amazing, heady days.

The only problems had come from the self-styled Hork-Bajir army led by that vile Andalite girl and Dak Hamee.

I had underestimated them both. Especially Dak Hamee. We took more and more Hork-Bajir who had been close to him, and when we opened their memories we learned about the Hork-Bajir "seer."

He had turned his people from peaceful, stupid herbivores into fearless and dangerous guerrilla fighters. I had not been able to catch the Andalite or the seer. I had not kept my promise to Akdor. But that no longer mattered. The great Akdor had been killed by a Hork-Bajir firing one of our own Dracon beams.

And then, our second very unpleasant surprise. A small fleet of Andalite ships had popped out of Zero-space, shockingly close to the Hork-Bajir world.

They had annihilated two of our ships in orbit. That's what had happened to Sub-Visser Fifteen. He'd been in charge of orbital defense. Sub-Visser Fifteen would die for his incompetence after a few more days of suffering.

Slowly we'd come to realize that this was not the full Andalite fleet. This was a task force. Just fighters and transports. Faster than our ships, but not as heavily armed. And we had ground bases.

"The Blade ship says they see the Andalites. Visser Four's orders are for all fighters to attack!"

"Of course those are his orders," I grumbled. "Let the Andalites chew up the fighters and then he can come in with his Blade ship, finish the battle, and claim all the glory." There was nothing I could do about it.

"Andalites," Alahar muttered unhappily. "Is it true that they control their ships with their thoughts?"

I sighed. "The Andalites are very advanced, very powerful, very determined. But they are not unbeatable. Prepare to go to full space normal speed. On my signal . . . NOW!"

We lit up our engines and hurtled along the arc of our orbit. Andalite ships ahead. My brother Yeerks all around us. The two fleets closed with shocking swiftness.

I took the weapons station. I fit my Hork-Bajir hands around the stick. "Be ready. The Andalites will close to within five thousand meters. Then they will break formation and attempt to dive beneath us so they can shoot upward into our bellies."

The Andalites came straight for us. Fifty thousand meters . . . forty thousand . . . thirty thousand . . . twenty thousand . . .

Some of the other Bug fighters were already firing, the fools. But at this range the Andalite defensive shields were too strong. The Andalite ships flared, shrugging off the energy.

Ten thousand meters . . . five thousand . . .

163

SHWWWOOOOOM!

The formation broke, just as I'd known it would. We were ready. I hit the altitude controls, dropped our nose, and fired!

TSEEEEEW! TSEEEEEW!

Twin beams of brilliant red light lanced toward the Andalite ship.

BOOOOM!

A hit! The Andalite fighter exploded into sizzling debris. I caught a split-second glance of an Andalite body hurtling by.

"Yes! Now do you see? They are not unbeatable!" All the hours of studying the enemy was paying off.

"Two of our Bug fighters destroyed," Alahar reported.

That cooled my excitement somewhat. Two-to-one in favor of the Andalites. But the one kill had been mine! "Bring the ship around, but take us out of this orbit. Take us down a few miles. Let's see if we can draw the Andalites within range of our ground bases."

"We have an Andalite fighter on our tail!"

Down we went, down and down, till I could look down into one valley and see the trees. The Andalite stayed with us.

"Evasive maneuvers!" I said.

TSEEEEW! TSEEEEW!

The shredders missed us by inches. We jigged left. We jigged right. But the Andalite pilot would not let go.

TSEEEEW! TSEEEEEW!

"Ahhh! Ahhh! We've been hit! We've been hit!"

"Give me a damage report, you coward!"

"Um . . . um . . . left Dracon beam is out. Right side is still working."

"Take us down . . . down to treetop level and head north along the valley."

We dropped into the valley. Trees flashed by on both sides. The blue mist below swirled in our wake.

The Andalite was on us . . . on us . . . setting up a shot . . .

A single, massively powerful Dracon beam lanced from the ground and hit the pursuing Andalite. In the viewscreen I saw the right side of his ship explode. The Andalite pilot was still alive, still fighting to get some control when his wrecked fighter hit a thousand-foot-tall tree.

"Take us back up!" I ordered.

Needless to say, Alahar was no longer so frightened or reluctant. We zoomed recklessly through the trees and back up toward space.

"I'm not showing *any* Andalite ships now," Alahar said.

"They've run!"

"Yes," he agreed. "I'm showing four disabled or destroyed Andalite ships. Seven of ours. Still almost two-to-one for them."

I nodded. "So it is. But unless they bring reinforcements very quickly, it will be enough."

chapter 30

DAK HAMEE

We were not saved by the Andalites. Instead the war simply intensified. The Andalite main fleet was on its way. But it would not arrive for a year.

From time to time new Andalite forces would show up. They were individual ships that had been on patrol and heard the call for help. A fighter here, a transport there, a few dozen more Andalite warriors to throw into the battles.

The Yeerks were forced out of my own valley. But they were strengthening everywhere else. The Andalite ships took to hiding in Zero-space, popping out of normal space until they were needed. They no longer had the power to remain in orbit and survive.

On the ground, Alloran led a valiant effort. But it was merely a holding action.

There were victories. But at the end of each passing week, there were fewer Andalites and more of my people enslaved.

After six months, the two thousand Andalite warriors had been reduced to four hundred. My forty-two Hork-Bajir warriors were now just twelve.

We estimated that there were now a hundred thousand Hork-Bajir-Controllers.

We hid among the Arn, for the most part. The Arn didn't like it, but they were helpless. Of course, the secret of the Arn was now well-known to the Yeerks. As Quatzhinnikon had predicted, the Yeerks discovered they could not successfully infest the Arn.

So the Yeerks used the Arn in other valleys as slave labor to mine their raw materials and to build Yeerk ships. When an Arn was injured or worn out, the Yeerks used them for target practice.

But the Arn in my valley were untouched. The Yeerks had made two attempts to invade the Deep of my valley. We had slaughtered them.

The Yeerks knew where we hid. And we knew that sooner or later they would come for us.

I stood on a balcony outside the Arn dwelling I now used as my home. I looked up, but I could not see Mother Sky. All I could see was the blue mist barrier, glowing like no sky could.

I looked down and saw the seething, molten core of my planet, hundreds of miles down. The far wall of the valley was only a thousand feet away at this point, and I could see Arn busily going about their daily routines. Here and there an Andalite would trot by, simply hopping over the Arn in its way.

There was one place where there always seemed to be two or three Andalites. At first glance they were just a couple of warriors talking, relaxing. But they, or others, had been in that same place for days.

<What are you thinking?> Aldrea asked me.

"What are those Andalites guarding?" I asked.

She came and stood beside me. She pressed her small, weak hand against my arm, as she often did. <What makes you think they're guarding anything?>

"Every hour of every day for the last two weeks there are at least two Andalites over there in that same location," I said.

<They don't look like they're guarding anything.>

"And yet they are there. Every day. Every night. Do you know what it means, Aldrea?"

<No. I don't.>

"I'm going for a walk."

<I'll come with you.>

I went back inside, then down a set of steps to the walkway level. Along the walkway, waiting patiently for the slow-moving Arn. I came to a bridge. The bridges were narrow, infrequent, usually

169

crowded, and fairly terrifying to Andalites, who were not at all used to heights.

They were never more than three feet wide. Even a Hork-Bajir raised in the trees found them intimidating.

Aldrea kept pace with me, steadfastly looking straight ahead and never down. We reached the far side and turned left to get back to the place the Andalites were guarding.

"Hello, friends," I said to the two overly casual warriors there. "We would like to go in there."

<Why would you want to go in there?> one of them asked. <Nothing in there for a Hork-Bajir to strain his brain over.>

The warrior looked past me, saw Aldrea, and nodded respectfully.

<Why are you guarding this place?> Aldrea asked.

The two warriors grew less casual. Their tails rose a few inches. Their hands drifted down toward their holstered shredders.

<Guarding? Who's guarding?>

"Will you allow us to enter?" I asked.

<Listen to me, genius, this isn't a place for you. Why don't you go find some tree branches to chew on?>

Genius. It was one of several sneering terms the Andalite warriors had for Hork-Bajir. I ignored it.

<Listen, you —> Aldrea began to yell.

I cut her off. "Simple question, friends. Will you allow us to enter? It only requires a yes or no answer. Yes or no?"

<Move along,> the warrior said coldly.

I turned and walked away. Aldrea came up beside me.

<I guess you have to expect that. The rudeness, I mean. These warriors are under constant pressure, constant danger, far from home. They aren't always going to be very sensitive.>

"Their insults mean nothing," I lied. "The fact that they are hiding something means something."

<Let's ask Alloran.>

"No. He gave the orders to guard that place. I guess we'll have to forget about it."

Aldrea jumped ahead and blocked me. <Don't lie to me, Dak. You're going to try and find out what's in there. You just don't trust me to help you.>

I was determined to remain calm. But I wasn't able. Instead I shouted. "We have fought side by side with your people and you Andalites still treat us like inferiors! Like errand-runners or servants or like idiot clowns to amuse you!"

<They didn't know who you are,> Aldrea said. <They figured you were just some regular Hork-Bajir.>

"Ah, yes. They assumed I was just one of the *stupid* Hork-Bajir. The simpleminded Hork-Bajir. The expendable, irrelevant, foolish Hork-Bajir."

<That's not what I meant.>

"Of course it's what you meant," I said bitterly. "You Andalites have more respect for the vicious Yeerks or the cowardly Arn than you have for the Hork-Bajir who fight and die at your sides. All that matters to your people is intelligence. Well, I've learned enough about Yeerk and Andalite and Arn intelligence to make me sick."

All this while, Arn were walking around us and even through my legs, ignoring us.

<You're upset. I understand that.>

I laughed. "You almighty Andalites. There is no limit to your arrogance, is there? Well, let me tell you something: We may be simple people. But we don't use biology to invent monsters. And we don't enslave other species. And we don't unleash a plague of parasites on the galaxy, endangering every other free species, and then go swaggering around like the lords of the universe. No, we're too simple for all that. We're too stupid to lie and manipulate. We're too stupid to be ruthless. We're too stupid to know how to build powerful weapons designed to annihilate our enemies. Until you came, Andalite, we were too stupid to know how to kill."

<That's quite a speech,> Aldrea said softly.

<You've been wanting to say all that for a long time, haven't you?>

The anger had burned itself out. I felt hollow. Not better, not relieved. Just empty and tired. "We were peaceful people, tending our trees, ignorant of our creators. Unaware of everyone else in the galaxy. Now look at us. Now look what has become of us. The despised children of the Arn. Slaves of the Yeerks. Tools of the Andalites."

Aldrea stood close to me and pressed her upper body against my chest. I put my arm carefully around her shoulders. We stood there on the walkway for a long time, blind to all who passed.

<I will help you find out what they are hiding,> Aldrea said. <Tonight, when the Arn are asleep.>

"You can't go against your own people," I said.

She looked at me then, with all her eyes. <Dak, I hope it never comes to a choice between my people and . . . and you. But if it does, I'll stand with you.>

I smiled. I appreciated what she'd said. But I didn't believe it.

chapter 31

ALDREA

I went to see Alloran without telling Dak. I asked him what was in the guarded room. He told me very coldly to mind my own business. Alloran had always been arrogant. Now, after months of hopeless battle, he was brutal, distant, and above all, exhausted.

I pleaded with him. I even took his hand in mine.

The morphing technology was still so new that most people didn't know how it worked. It never occurred to Alloran, as he felt the strange calm and lethargy steal over him, that I was acquiring his DNA.

I rejoined Dak in the quarters we remnants of the Hork-Bajir army had taken. <I'm ready,> I said.

"You went to see Alloran," Dak said.

I was surprised. I saw Delf Hajool, Jagil's partner, looking ashamed. Jagil himself refused to look at me.

<Dak, you don't have to use Jagil and Delf to

spy on me. I went to Alloran for a reason. I acquired him.>

That surprised him. I got some small pleasure out of his expression.

"The morphing technology? But he must know what you did. His warriors must have seen."

I went over to Delf and took her claw hand in mine. <It was just like this, Dak. Alloran felt a momentary peace and calm. As Delf is now feeling. No one watching would even know.> I released Delf's hand.

Dak nodded. He even smiled. "Good plan."

<We do want to get in without anyone getting hurt,> I said.

It was so easy morphing Alloran that I barely knew it was happening. There was no mental change. I still had the same Andalite instincts. But now, as I walked ahead of Dak, I felt the increased physical power of being in a male form. When I turned my stalk eyes back, I saw the heavy tail blade of a male. I also felt the slight male clumsiness, the lack of subtle balance that a female Andalite possesses.

I marched steadily, unswerving, unhesitating, toward the guarded door. The guards saw me coming, straightened their pose, and stopped talking.

<Report,> I said. I halfway expected the guards

to burst out laughing at me. I may have looked and sounded like Alloran, but I didn't feel like him.

<Nothing new since . . . well, since this Hork-Bajir here, or one who looks just like him, came by with Seerow's daughter today.>

<Different Hork-Bajir,> I said. <But then, they do all look alike. Open up.>

<Yes, War-Prince Alloran. But the Hork-Bajir?>

I turned my stalk eyes on him. <Are you questioning me?>

<No! No, War-Prince Alloran. Not at all.>

The door opened. The guards stepped aside. <Stay out here. Watch for the girl. She may come back.>

We went inside. It was a medium-sized room. I saw no Andalites, no Arn. The room was filled with equipment, machinery, much of it glowing and flashing. It was an eerie scene.

"What is all this?" Dak asked.

<I have no idea,> I admitted. <Some of this is Andalite, but I believe most of it is Arn.> I went over to something I recognized: an Andalite computer panel.

<Computer on,> I said.

<Identify user,> the computer's thought-speak voice requested.

I took a deep breath to drive away the fluttering in my stomach. <Alloran-Semitur-Corrass,> I said.

<Thought-speak identification confirmed. Ready,> the computer said.

<We will be in very serious trouble if we get caught,> I said.

Dak smiled. "Aldrea, we've been in trouble since we first met."

<Computer, identify the purpose of this facility.>

Fortunately, computers don't understand the concept of a suspicious question. The computer answered.

<This facility uses Arn biotechnology matched with Andalite computer technology to formulate and produce biological specimens.>

I frowned. <What biological specimens?>

<Onkalillium . . .>

<That's an organic medicine,> I told Dak.

<And Virus Q-One-Eighteen.>

My hearts skipped a beat. Why would anyone be creating a virus?

<Explain the exact purpose of Virus Q-One-Eighteen.>

<Virus Q-One-Eighteen is a Quantum virus. It is designed to attack a specific type of living creature at the subatomic level, bypassing all possible countermeasures. It is designed to cause death within minutes.>

<No,> I whispered.

"Ask it what 'specific type of living creature'?" Dak demanded.

For a moment, I just couldn't do it. I just couldn't, because the computer would answer. The computer would tell the truth, and I couldn't hear the truth.

"Ask it!" Dak snapped.

<Computer, what species is Virus Q-One-Eighteen designed to attack?>

<Hork-Bajir.>

chapter 32

DAK HAMEE

We stood there, the two of us, motionless. I don't know what Aldrea felt. I know what I felt.

I was angry, filled with rage at the Andalites for having done this evil thing.

But beneath the rage was such sadness. Such awful sadness. All for nothing. All the fighting, the killing. For what? The Andalites had seen the truth: We had lost. The Hork-Bajir people would be slaves of the Yeerks.

This virus was an admission of failure. The Andalites couldn't save the Hork-Bajir. So rather than let them fall into Yeerk hands, they would annihilate them.

<I didn't know,> Aldrea said. <I didn't know. This is wrong. This is wrong. They can't do this.>

"It makes perfect sense," I said. "To the brilliant, ruthless mind of an Andalite, it makes perfect sense. They would rather destroy us than have us become tools of the Yeerks."

179

<No!> Aldrea cried with more force than I'd ever heard from her. <No! That is *not* how we are. Alloran has lost his mind. The Electorate will never support this. Never!>

"Maybe not," I said. "But the Andalite Electorate is not here. Alloran is."

<We are not going to let this happen,> Aldrea said. <We are Andalites. We do not destroy sentient species.>

"What can we do?" I shrugged helplessly at the rows of flashing and glowing machines all around me.

<Computer!> Aldrea snapped. <Can you place all the Q-One-Eighteen produced so far in one container small enough to carry safely?>

<Yes.>

<Then do it!>

"What are you going to do, Aldrea?"

<I'm going to destroy the virus and destroy this laboratory.>

"You'd be going against your own people!"

She began to change, to morph out of Alloran's form back into her own. She then looked at me through her own eyes again and spoke with her own silent voice. <No. *My* people do not wipe out entire populations. *My* people came to protect the Hork-Bajir, not to destroy them. I don't know what

Alloran has become, but he is not one of *my* people.>

"Alloran and his warriors will try and stop us."

<Yes. I know.>

I smiled, despite everything. Alloran had failed us. My people were doomed now, either way. But in the end, Aldrea was my true friend. She had lied to me, used me from time to time, and yet now, here, in this black moment, she was my true friend.

"I didn't believe you," I admitted. "When you said if you were forced to choose, you'd choose me."

<Of course you didn't believe it,> Aldrea said. <I was lying. Once again. But this isn't a choice at all. This can't be allowed to happen.>

"You and I alone, going against the Yeerks *and* the Andalites," I said.

Aldrea nodded. <I guess that is true.>

"Then from now on, no more lies. No more manipulation. No more Andalite subtlety."

Aldrea nodded. <Let's just hope that "from now on" lasts longer than the next few minutes.>

She pointed at a shining, steel cylinder that had risen dramatically from a console. <That must be the virus. Would you mind carrying it? Your arms are stronger than mine.>

I lifted the deadly cylinder. Aldrea drew her shredder.

<Be ready to run,> she said, and raised the shredder.

I'd seen many brave deeds since the war had begun. But none braver than that. The Andalite girl turning against her own people to save mine.

I cared very much for her then. I probably had before that, but that was when I finally realized it. With all her lies, all her inbred Andalite arrogance, all her manipulations, I loved her.

<Let's blow this place up.>

She began firing, and I didn't have time to think, only act.

TSEEEEW! TSEEEEW!

Consoles exploded. Machinery melted. The room was instantly as hot as sun on the highest branches.

TSEEEEW! TSEEEEW!

Buh-BOOOM!

The guards came rushing in.

WHUMPF! I hit one on the side of his head using the canister. He went down, unconscious.

Aldrea calmly shifted the shredder, dialed down the power, and shot the other guard with a low-power blast that left him stunned and stupid on the floor.

<That should be sufficient damage,> Aldrea said. <Let's get out of here!>

We ran outside, with me dragging the two Andalites out of harm's way. The room kept exploding in showers of sparks and sudden arcs of megavoltage.

I cradled the container and Aldrea led the way. Down the walkway we raced. The city was empty and as dark as it ever got with the low glow from the core. All the Arn were asleep.

But then the front wall of the laboratory exploded. The sound echoed all around the valley. No one was asleep after that.

<Out onto the bridge!> Aldrea cried. <We'll throw the canister into the Deep. It should burn up safely that way.>

We turned to head out onto the bridge. But the Andalites had reacted quickly to the sound of the explosion. Andalite warriors were pouring from their quarters.

I saw Alloran appear on the far side of the valley. He was unmistakable, even from a thousand feet away. And even from that distance he realized what was happening.

<Stop them!> he cried in a thought-speak roar.

Andalites rushed onto the bridge from the far side. Andalites were coming up behind us on the walkway.

Trapped!

And then . . .

TSEEEEW! TSEEEEW!

Down the length of the valley, three Bug fighters swooped, firing their Dracon beams. The sonic boom of their passing shook the stone beneath my feet.

TSEEEEW! TSEEEEW!

Dracon beams ripped open the stone walls like an arm blade going through rain-soaked *Stoola* bark.

Andalite defenses, shredder cannon mounted above walkways, fired back. The valley erupted in blistering light and explosions. Everywhere shredders and Dracon beams fired. Everywhere the stones cracked and shattered and exploded into pebbles.

TSEEEEW! TSEEEEW!

Three more Bug fighters were coming in, fast as the first flight, firing just as madly. Groggy Arn were dying by the hundreds. Furious Andalites were being hit by flying rock and by direct Dracon beam fire.

Kah-BOOOOOM! Shredder cannon hit a Bug fighter! It blew open on one side, careened wildly, then slammed into a wall.

"Yaahhhh!" I cheered. Madness! I was cheering the Andalites who would destroy us.

We began to run out onto the bridge. We still had to destroy the canister. But a Dracon beam slashed across my path, stopping me in my tracks. I was half-blinded by the flash.

We had been temporarily forgotten by the Andalites who rushed to their weapons. Forgotten by all but one Andalite.

When I could see again, Alloran was halfway across the bridge, coming toward us, oblivious to the danger.

He was a brave Andalite, racing across that narrow span miles above the red-hot core of the planet, with Yeerk Bug fighters zooming literally feet above his head. He was brave, yes. That I had to acknowledge. But I would see him dead before I would let him use his virus against my people.

<It's over, Alloran,> Aldrea cried. <You are not going to destroy the Hork-Bajir!>

<I'm trying to save this planet, you fool!> Alloran said.

<Will you save it by destroying it?>

<Give me that canister,> Alloran warned.

He was almost across. Other Andalites were responding again to his orders by blocking us from behind. We could no longer hope to get far enough out on the bridge to drop the canister into the Deep.

We were trapped, and now, down the length of the valley, came a ship whose very appearance struck fear in me. Andalite shredder cannon fired, but the Blade ship's shields turned the attacks into harmless light shows.

On it came, much slower than the Bug fighters, huge and invulnerable. Its very slowness was insolent, a slap in the face of the Andalites who could not harm it.

The Blade ship fired.

TSEEEEEW! TSEEEEW!

The bridge exploded before me, opening up a gap a hundred feet across. Alloran on one side. Me and Aldrea on the other.

<Kill them!> Alloran ordered his warriors. <Kill that Hork-Bajir, and kill that treasonous spawn of Seerow's, too!>

The Blade ship approached, firing and flying low.

The Andalite warriors leveled their shredders at Aldrea and me. They looked confused, doubtful. Would they obey their battle-maddened prince?

Aldrea turned her face to me. She took my free hand in hers. <We tried,> she said simply.

But I was not ready to die. Not just yet. The Blade ship came on, flying low. I tightened my grip on Aldrea's hand. "Jump!"

<What?>

"Trust me. Jump!"

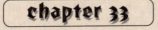

chapter 33

ALDREA

We jumped into shadow.

We fell.

THUMP! Bump!

<Owww!>

We landed on the Blade ship as it passed beneath the shattered bridge. I tried to stand. But my right front leg was broken. The pain waited a few moments before hitting with such severity that I almost fainted.

Dak was lying beside me, unconscious on the black metal-composite skin of the ship.

The Blade ship rose up from the valley, up past the wall cities of the Arn, all crumbled and in flames now. Up we rose through the blue mist.

<Dak! Dak! Wake up! This thing is going to accelerate in a few seconds!>

He opened his eyes. "Are we above the Deep? Can I throw this canister?"

<I can't be sure,> I said. <You may end up dropping it into the trees!>

He jumped to his feet. We were above the mist, over the sloping valley floor. The crowns of trees were marching past on our right and our left. The ship would accelerate any moment, going from this crawling pace to many times the speed of sound to gain altitude before a second pass down the valley.

"One more jump," Dak said. He ran over, staggering on the moving, uneven surface of the ship. He handed me the canister. "Hold this tight!" Then he scooped me up, lifting me beneath my belly.

Dak jumped, slinging my weight along with him. He reached out a hand in the darkness and grabbed the crown of a tree. We swung, swung, swung, with the treetop bending way over, tossing us around like a spring.

"Can you morph the *chadoo*?" Dak asked, grunting from the effort of holding me.

<Yes. But what about the canister? I'll drop it. The *chadoo*'s arms aren't strong enough. Wait. I have a different idea.>

I began to morph. I began to morph the one creature that could swing in the trees and still hold the deadly canister safely.

"What are you doing?" Dak cried as my body changed in his arms.

<Morphing. Just hold on, it will only take a few minutes.>

I felt my tail shorten and thicken. It lost its suppleness and strength and became a sort of dead third leg.

I felt my front legs wither and shrink away, as my hind legs strengthened and grew large, clawed feet. I felt incredible new strength in my arms. They thickened, piling muscle on muscle.

My stalk eyes went dark and then hardened to form the big, forward-raked horns.

And then, on my arms, on my legs, the blades began to emerge.

"You're morphing a Hork-Bajir!"

"Yes," I said, using the Hork-Bajir mouth. "I acquired Delf."

I clutched the canister tightly. I reached for the treetop and gripped it with my Hork-Bajir claw.

"We're in this together, Dak. If the Quantum virus is released, now I will die, too."

"I don't want that!"

"I do, Dak. I'll live or die with you."

Then Dak pressed his forehead horns to mine, and I felt the tingle of a sensation I had not guessed Hork-Bajir could feel. It was a Hork-Bajir kiss, I suppose. What we Andalites do when we stroke another's face with our palms.

189

We hung there from the crown of a thousand-foot-tall tree and for a moment, at least, forgot about the battle raging, and the war lost, and the canister that contained so much destruction.

At last, we swung down the tree, down to the ground.

And there, surrounding us on all sides, stood a small army of Hork-Bajir. All were armed with Dracon beam weapons. All those weapons were pointed at us.

One Hork-Bajir stepped forward.

"Dak Hamee, Hork-Bajir seer, and no less than Aldrea, the daughter of Seerow," he said. "I do love this new Andalite morphing technology. It was fascinating to watch. It will be even more fascinating to use, once I have made you my host."

ESPLIN 9466

Did I gloat a little? Oh, yes. Oh, yes indeed.

"Allow me to introduce myself," I said. "My name is Esplin-Nine-Four-Double-Six. My rank is Sub-Visser Twelve, although with this triumph I think my rank is very, very likely to be elevated. Ah, yes, this will be a great success."

"Enjoy it while you can, Yeerk. You won't live long enough to see another promotion."

I smiled down at the transformed Andalite girl. "We met before, of course. That was the first time I saw your morphing ability at work. This time I was able to watch from one of the many sensors we've strung through the trees. Very impressive. It will make owning an Andalite host all that more desirable. Take them!"

My warriors leaped forward and grabbed the two rebels. We shackled their hands behind them and dragged them to my fighter parked a few hundred yards away.

"Careful with them," I scolded one of my warriors after he kicked Dak Hamee. "Those are our bodies. We don't want them damaged."

I glanced over at the canister they carried. It was sealed. It looked dangerous. I considered opening it to look inside. But some sense of caution warned me to leave it alone. I handed it to one of my warriors to carry.

The fighter was too small to fit all my guards, so I kept two. They stood with Dracon beams leveled at the captives as we took off. I was going to rendezvous with the Blade ship after having shot up the Andalite's refuge.

But the Blade ship was not back in orbit yet. They were having too much fun frying the Andalites in the Deep, I suppose.

So we waited. No matter how much glory anyone else had from the battle with the Andalites, I had fulfilled my promise to capture or kill the Andalite girl and the Hork-Bajir leader.

Best of all, I had the first and only captive Andalite.

"Why not morph back to your own form?" I said to her. "There is no point in trying to deceive me."

"I know what you want," Aldrea said. "I'm not going to give it to you."

"You can't possibly stay in that form forever," I said.

"Yes, I can," Aldrea said. "In fact, in an hour and a half, I'll have no choice. I'll be Hork-Bajir permanently."

There was no doubting the truth of what she said. She said it too triumphantly for it to be a lie.

"There's a time limit?" I demanded.

"Yes," she said with a sneer. "There is."

"What is in the canister?" I asked.

"Open it and see," Dak Hamee said.

"Oh, aren't we just the defiant young heroes?" I mocked them. "Very brave."

I walked over to Dak Hamee. I smiled at Aldrea. And I kicked Dak as hard as I could. Then I kicked him again. He groaned and fell over, facedown on the deck.

"Demorph, Andalite," I said.

"NO!" the fool Hork-Bajir yelled. "Don't let him —"

I kicked him again.

"Demorph, Andalite. I don't want to bruise my foot hurting your friend. Just demorph. It doesn't matter. You will both become host bodies, like it or not. So why endure the pain?"

Then it occurred to me. The realization blossomed in my head like the loveliest flower. Of course! Of *course*!

"Grab her. Hold her down!" I cried, ecstatic at the idea in my head. "I don't need her to demorph.

I can infest her now and then force her to demorph! Hah-hah-hah!"

My warriors rushed forward. They grabbed her head. They twisted her ear around.

"NO!"

Dak Hamee bellowed and struggled, but the shackles held him tight.

I began to release my hold on the Hork-Bajir brain of my host body. I slithered out, pressing myself down to move quickly out of the Hork-Bajir ear. For a horrible long moment I was blind, connected to neither host.

But then I sensed the new Hork-Bajir ear, the one that was only a morph of the Andalite inside. I squeezed through. I reached desperately with my palps, reaching for contact.

I was still hanging half out of the Andalite's ear when I touched her brain and felt her mind. It was a shock. There it was, a Hork-Bajir brain physically, but within it was not the idiot Hork-Bajir mind, but the lightning-fast Andalite intelligence.

I saw inside the mind, the memories of Aldrea, the Andalite. I saw it all in a flash! All that she had been, all that she had done to thwart us. I saw the secret of the canister.

But most of all, I saw her running, tail high, four eyes open, seeing in all directions at once. Running free across the grass of the Andalite home.

<Hello, Andalite!> I cried, sensing that she was aware of me in her mind. <You are mine! My host! My slave!>

I could not wait to get completely wrapped around her brain. I had to see inside her memories, all of them. And I opened my own mind and memories, too, letting her see all that I was, all that I had been. I wanted her to fear me, to understand how hopeless her life was now.

<Yes, look into my mind, Andalite. Do you see who I am? Do you see that I am your master? Do you realize now how we will crush you, crush you all?>

I touched the area that controlled sight. I opened one Hork-Bajir eye. I saw Dak Hamee, shouting, struggling. I saw my two guards watching, fascinated. In a moment I would demorph and make the first ever Andalite-Controller! Then they would gape! Then the entire Yeerk race would . . .

A movement! Another Hork-Bajir. But who . . . my own host body!

Time seemed to stand frozen, as I realized the depths of my mistake. My former host body was no longer under control.

Noooooooo! I cried silently. *Noooooooo!*

My host body, free now, drew back one arm and brought it down on the neck of one of my guards. My warrior dropped like a stone. The other warrior

195

spun around, but too slow, too clumsy. My former host dispatched him, too.

And then, as I struggled helplessly to finish taking control of the Andalite and get safely inside her head, I felt a hand close around my lower body.

I was being pulled out! Noooo! Noooo!

My palps lost contact with the eyes. My palps lost contact with the Andalite mind.

I was blind again! Helpless. I felt an impact as I hit the deck.

I knew my life would end.

And yet in my powerless rage, there was a part of me that still could think of nothing but that sweet memory. Of the overwhelming beauty of an Andalite running free.

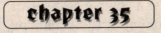

chapter 35

DAK HAMEE

The Yeerk slug lay helpless on the deck. Two Hork-Bajir-Controllers lay there, too.

"Who are you?" I asked the Hork-Bajir who had been Esplin's host.

"I am Gah Fillat," he said. "You are Dak Hamee. You are different."

I smiled. "Not so different. Can you help me remove these shackles?"

Gah looked concerned. He looked confused. He was, after all, one of my people. He had never known the word "shackle." He'd had no reason to know it.

"I can do it," Aldrea said. She crawled to one of the unconscious Hork-Bajir-Controllers. She pulled his Dracon beam from his hand and used it to burn away the shackles.

"Are you all right?" I asked her.

She nodded. "I am now."

But there was something wrong with her. I

could tell. Something had changed. She noticed me staring.

"The Yeerk. Esplin-Nine-Four-Double-Six. I saw inside his memories," she said. "I guess . . . I guess nothing is ever as simple as it seems."

I looked down at the squirming, writhing slug. So harmless now. So helpless.

I hated him. Hated him and all his race for what they had done to my people. But I did not want to kill him. I was just tired. Too tired to draw breath.

"What shall we do?" Aldrea asked me.

"With him?" I nodded at the Yeerk. "I don't know."

"Not just with him," Aldrea said. "With every-thing. With us. We could use this Bug fighter. We could fly far away. Find some uninhabited planet. Leave this place forever."

"Is that what you want to do?" I asked her.

"I am Hork-Bajir now. We could be . . . we could be *us*."

I reached for her and took her hand. "Maybe there —"

BOOOOM!

The ship was spinning out of control. There were flames. I was thrown against the deck, the ceiling, the walls. Everything spun madly.

Through the window I caught glimpses of a ship

firing at us again. Not a Yeerk ship. An Andalite fighter.

It had spotted us. We were a Bug fighter. It was attacking. And it had already crippled the fighter. The air was almost gone. My lungs were sucking on nothing.

Aldrea fought her way to the controls. Gasping, crying, she struggled with the Yeerk control panel, slammed by the flying bodies of the unconscious Hork-Bajir-Controllers. She was having trouble using thick Hork-Bajir fingers instead of her own Andalite hands.

Down we went. The spinning slowed, but down we went.

"We're going to crash!" Aldrea screamed.

WHAM! BUMP!

The side of the ship tore off. I saw flashes of trees! We hit again and again.

Then, suddenly, we stopped moving.

I raised my head, then lost consciousness.

When I woke again, I saw Aldrea bleeding.

Again, I lost consciousness.

It was daylight when I next opened my eyes. I looked up into Aldrea's face. Only it was Delf's face, of course.

"You are Hork-Bajir now," I said stupidly, my mind groggy and confused.

"Forever," she said. "The time limit has passed. I am Hork-Bajir."

My head began to clear. Memories returned. "The others?"

"The two Hork-Bajir-Controllers are gone," she said. "Our friend Gah Fillat is hunting for bark."

"And the Yeerk? Esplin-Nine-Four-Double-Six?"

She shrugged. "I looked. I didn't find him. There's a stream just over there. Maybe . . ."

I stood up. My head felt like it had been pummeled by a *Jubba-Jubba*. But I was alive. And Aldrea was alive. And . . .

"The canister!" I cried.

Aldrea's eyes opened wide. "I forgot about it!"

We both ran to the wreckage of the Bug fighter. It was strewn across several hundred feet. Sheet composite and even an entire engine hung in the branches above us.

We searched for half an hour. Then a voice called out, "Dak Hamee, I am here!"

It was Gah. He was in the tree above us, in the high branches. He was swinging down to meet us. He was carrying the canister. He had retrieved it from the branches above. He had known that it was important. He was bringing it to us.

"No," Aldrea whispered. "No, no, no!"

The canister top was open.

"Run, Dak! We have to run! The wind is blowing it from us, but we have to run!"

"Gah!" I cried. "Gah Fillat!" But what could I say to him? There was nothing I could do. As I watched in horror, his face twisted, his eyes bulged.

We ran.

We ran and ran.

We ran down the valley, down toward our temporary home among the Arn. We had nowhere else to go.

We ran through the blue mist, down to the edge of the cliff. Smoke billowed up from the wall-city. I heard distant cries. The voices of the Arn.

And as we stood there, we saw an Andalite fighter rise up through the smoke. Behind it, a transport. Another fighter. The second transport. All that was left of the Andalite task force.

We stood there watching as they rose, up and up, gaining speed. They disappeared into the blue mist. Watching the last of our pathetic hopes evaporate.

We stood there on the edge of that cliff, knowing the Quantum virus was spreading on the wind, and knowing that the Andalites were leaving forever.

The end had come. The war was lost.

"It's over," Aldrea said. "The Andalites are gone. The Hork-Bajir are doomed."

But even now, I was not ready to surrender. Yes, the Andalites were gone. But surely there was still some hope. Surely there had to be *some* hope for my people.

"There are valleys the virus will not reach for a time," I said. "Some will survive. Surely some will survive. And . . . and there are still the trees."

"And us," Aldrea said. "For now, for a while, we will have us."

We stood there for a long time. The passing of the Andalite ships had left swirls in the blue mist. But then the swirls were gone. All that remained were the pillars of smoke and the faint cries of those who had created my people.

And in orbit, and in all the valleys, and in the very heads of my people, there were the Yeerks.

I was Dak Hamee. Hork-Bajir seer. But I could not see the future. I could not see the hope I knew must still be there.

But I could see Aldrea. Different now, a Hork-Bajir. And yet still Aldrea. I could see her. And that would be enough.

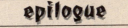

epilogue

Jara Hamee's voice fell silent.

I ruffled my wings to shake the morning dew from them. The fire was gone, not even embers now. The Hork-Bajir had all gone to sleep long ago.

All but Jara Hamee. They'd all heard the story before.

<That's an amazing story,> I said to Jara Hamee. <Not exactly a happy one, though.>

"Yes. Good story. Sad story," Jara said. "Jara Hamee tell. Father tell Jara Hamee. Father-father tell father. I tell daughter."

He looked fondly at the young Hork-Bajir who had curled up beside her mother in the night.

<Your *daughter*? I still can't always tell male Hork-Bajir from female Hork-Bajir,> I admitted. <But what's the end of the story? You didn't tell me the end.>

"Story have no end," Jara said, laughing like I was a great fool. "Stories go on."

<I guess you're right. Besides, I guess I don't

want to know the next part of that story. It was pretty sad. Too easy to see my own people going the way of the Hork-Bajir. Still, I wish I knew what became of Dak and Aldrea. And even Esplin-Nine-Four-Double-Six.>

"Jara know that. Dak Hamee and Aldrea daughter of Seerow live. Have child. Then die."

<The child was your father?>

"Yes." Once again, Jara looked at me like I was dense. "Dak and Aldrea have son. Son called Seerow. In honor of Seerow. Not Hork-Bajir name."

<No, I kind of figured that out.>

"Son Seerow have son. That son, Jara Hamee!"

<Well. There you go, then. And Esplin-Nine-Four-Double-Six?>

Jara looked slyly at me. "Tobias knows Esplin-Nine-Four-Double-Six."

Yes. Of course, I did. The Yeerk who was obsessed by Andalites. The Yeerk who had managed to survive despite everything.

<Visser Three?>

"Visser Three."

I sighed. I had come to the Hork-Bajir looking to feel better. Now I was more depressed than before. And I was sleepy. And hungry.

It wasn't a good story for a person already wondering what the point of his life was. The Yeerks had won. Evil had triumphed. The Hork-Bajir, all except this small band, were enslaved.

The Hork-Bajir began waking up, stirring, opening their eyes. They were probably stiff from lying in these unaccustomed positions on the ground. After all, they were used to life in the trees.

Ket Halpak woke up and smiled at me. Her daughter did not smile, just looked at me curiously.

<Thanks for telling me the story, Jara,> I said. <I guess . . . I guess we can hope that someday there will be another great Hork-Bajir seer like Dak Hamee. Maybe he'll be luckier, huh?>

"Yes," Jara Hamee said.

"Yes," Ket Halpak agreed.

I opened my wings, ready to catch the breeze.

"Tobias," Jara said. "This daughter named Toby. Name for Tobias."

<Wow. That's an honor, Jara and Ket.> I was really touched. It was a typically sweet Hork-Bajir thing to do. <But it's kind of a strange name for a Hork-Bajir, isn't it?>

"Yes," Ket agreed. "Strange name."

"Good name," Jara said. "Toby is different."

"Yes," Ket agreed, "Toby is different."

I smiled to myself and caught the breeze beneath my wings. But then, just as I lifted off, I felt the strangest tingling sensation. I veered back and floated above the Hork-Bajir.

<When you say Toby is different . . .>

Jara and Ket didn't answer. Instead, the Hork-Bajir girl herself looked up at me and smiled a very serious smile. "Yes, Tobias, friend of the Hork-Bajir. Yes, I am *different*."

The wind picked me up then, and I soared up and away. But with my hawk's eyes I watched them for a long time. And at some point, I started feeling really good. I felt happy because Jara Hamee was right. Stories have no end. And my namesake, Toby Hamee, the descendant of a brave Andalite girl and a Hork-Bajir seer, was going to write the next chapter.

About the Author

K.A. Applegate is the author of over 100 books for middle-grade readers and young adults including the best-selling Animorphs series. Ms. Applegate was born in Michigan and has lived in many regions of the United States, including Texas, Florida, California, and Minnesota. She has recently moved to Chicago, where she divides her time between writing, reading, and vegging out in front of the tube.

According to Ms. Applegate, "*The Hork-Bajir Chronicles* is a book I've wanted to write for a long time. I wanted to show that most stories of conflict are more complicated than any one side would have you believe. Not that good and evil are impossible to find or define, just that reality is usually a little grayer around the edges."

Speak Now or Forever Hold Your Peace.

ANIMORPHS

K. A. Applegate

Something is driving Marco insane. Something personal. The stress is so bad that it's affecting his ability to morph. The problem? His dad has been dating, and now marriage is on the horizon. Marco knows that his mother might still be alive. But how can he possibly tell his dad the truth?

ANIMORPHS #35: THE PROPOSAL

Coming in October

Watch TV ANIMORPHS on NICKELODEON

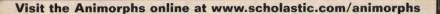

Have you experienced the changes online?

ANIMORPHS™

Up-to-the-minute info
on the Animorphs!

Sneak previews
of books and
TV episodes!

Contests!

Fun downloads
and games!

Messages from
K.A. Applegate

See what other fans
are saying on the Forum!

Check out the official Animorphs Web site at:
www.scholastic.com/animorphs

It'll change the way you see things.